THE LETTER

Antonio Giannini
1103 Middlecreek
Seattle, Washington 98101

Rabbi Mark Davidson
Rabbinical Council of America
New York, NY 10001

Jerry Yellin

TotalRecall Publications, Inc.

United States of America,

Canada and United Kingdom

To Tom

To live in Unity with all of Humanity, in Harmony
with all of Nature and find Peace on our Planet.

Prologue

The letter addressed to Rabbi Mark Davidson, Rabbinical Council of America, New York, NY, arrived on June 10. It was from Antonio Giannini, an attorney in Seattle, Washington. It read:

Dear Rabbi Davidson,

I represent a woman from this area named Pat Meisenger who passed away a few days ago in Bellingham. Last year when she learned of her terminal illness, she wrote a letter to your father, Samuel Davidson, regarding a brief encounter she had with him on Iwo Jima in 1945 and the impact that encounter had on her life. She entrusted me with her letter and instructed me to send it to your father upon her demise. However, in view of Mr. Davidson's age and physical condition, I have taken it upon myself to deviate from her wishes and contact you instead.

I will adhere to her instructions and forward the letter to you only upon your request. You may contact me at the address above or by email, fax, or phone per the numbers on this letterhead.

Very truly yours,
Antonio Giannini, Esq.

Rabbi Mark Davidson could not imagine what could have happened between his father, Judge Samuel Davidson, and a woman sixty-one years ago that would have a deleterious effect on him if he found out now. Judge Davidson was eighty-two, in good health, had all of his mental faculties, and did not shock easily. As an attorney and judge, he had seen, heard, and been part of many bizarre cases and experiences. The Rabbi was inclined to pass this letter on to his father and let him deal with it in his own way. His training as a Rabbi always made him think how best to stay out of people's private affairs and guide them to self-made decisions. This, he determined, might not be a situation that would allow him to do that, so he decided to call Mr. Giannini.

Their conversation was cordial at first. Mr. Giannini knew about Rabbi Davidson through the prominence of his father, Judge Davidson, and the little publicity the Rabbi had generated about himself as an outspoken proponent of women's rights and other issues unpopular with the current administration in Washington. At first, Mark was suspicious of Mr. Giannini's tone. However, the talk became much friendlier when Mr. Giannini volunteered that he was in agreement with much of what the Rabbi thought and stood for.

"I never read the letter, Rabbi; I only know that my client had written it recently. I was asked to represent her by a former priest from my Parish. I know the letter is quite lengthy and the sealed package may also include a few pictures." Mark asked him to mail it the next post and he said he would send it Fed-Ex that afternoon.

Two days later the package arrived at Mark's office. Mark found it on his desk when he returned from visiting congregants in the hospital. It was late afternoon and he did not know if he had the energy to finish writing his sermon, and then read what might be a difficult letter, before leaving for home. Curious, he opened the package. Attached to the outside of the envelope addressed to Samuel Davidson was a small, faded picture of his father as a twenty one year old fighter pilot with a young woman. "Pat and Sam, July 9, 1945, Iwo Jima" was inscribed on the back of the photo. His hands began to tremble as he held the picture, and he wondered if he was doing the right thing. Should his father be opening and reading the letter? Should he have held off having the package sent, or even ignored Mr. Giannini's letter? As these questions bounced around in his head, he carefully opened the envelope and felt the heft of the typewritten pages.

The Letter

Dear Samuel, I am writing this letter to you 60 years after I should have written it and after years of hesitation. What prompted me to do it now is the knowledge that I have only a few more months to live and I felt that you should know the impact our brief encounter had on my life. I really do not even know if you will remember me after all this time, so I have attached a picture that I have held close to my heart ever since it was taken on July 9, 1945. I remember the date so well; it was the day after I arrived at your airfield on Iwo Jima as part of a small USO troop called the Winged Pigeons. There were four of us, two girls and two guys, musicians and dancers sent to forward bases to entertain as best we could and bring a little home to the soldiers.

We watched as your squadron returned from a mission over Japan. What a thrilling sight it was as you buzzed that dirt airfield, peeled off in groups of four and landed. That evening I was walking along the flight line and you were sitting on the wing of your P-51, smoking a cigarette, and staring at Mt. Suribachi. I had never seen a more forlorn look on such a young, handsome man. I stopped, jangled your foot and when you looked down I said,

"Hi, I'm Pat Meisenger from Bellingham, Washington, how are you?" You seemed to come out of a trance, jumped down, stuck out your hand, and said, "Sam Davidson from Newark, nice to meet you."

I wanted to know more, so I asked, "Who is Lilly D?", the name on the side of your airplane. That began a conversation and led to a walk to a burnt out pillbox overlooking the ocean. We were on top of that pillbox all night while you told me about Lillian, your plans to get married, the mission you had flown that day and the loss of your two squadron mates, Al Sherren and Pudgy Carr. You were so sad. My heart filled with an overwhelming desire to hold you, console you. When I moved closer, you responded to my touch. We made love that night and I felt gratified that I had given myself to you even though I knew that it was my prompting, not you that made it happen.

I flew to Guam the next afternoon and did not return to the States until mid-August, the day before the war ended. I returned to Bellingham a few days later and discovered I was pregnant. My family raised me as a Catholic and I believed all that I had learned and practiced my entire life. I knew that my condition would destroy my mother and father and my oldest brother who was a priest. I knew that I had to deliver my child, our child, and I knew that I could not tell you or keep the baby. Perhaps it was a mistake not trying to find you and tell *you after the baby boy was born, or even asking if you and Lillian wanted him, but that is not what I did. I also knew that I could not stay in Bellingham so I told my family that I was going back on the road with a USO troupe and flew to San Diego where my cousin Katherine lived.*

Her new name was Katherine Meisenger Flowers; she had married a Marine officer in 1942. Her husband, Barry, was the scion of a very wealthy, influential Texas family. His wounds from the battle on Iwo Jima were devastating and he was recovering at the Naval Hospital in San Diego. The doctors told Kate that he would be OK in time, but he might not be able to have children.

I called Kate, told her I was pregnant, and asked her if she and Barry might take my baby. Kate was very excited and when Barry said yes but with conditions, I moved in with Kate to wait for the birth. Barry's conditions were in line with his and his family's very strong feelings about religion. They were fundamentalist Christians to the core with strong anti-Catholic and Jewish prejudices. I was desperate and agreed that I would give birth without revealing who the father was. Kate had to agree that if she and Barry were ever divorced that Barry would retain the baby and it would not be raised as a Catholic. Worst of all, Kate, and I would not be able to have any contact. Had I known all of this beforehand I might not have consented to the arrangement with Kate and Barry.

Kate told me that she heard Barry's father Peter say to him "There are only two good Jews in Texas, Neiman and Marcus, and if it wasn't for that Jew-loving Roosevelt you wouldn't be sitting in a wheelchair but would be down on the ranch chasing woman like I did at your age and becoming a man." Can you imagine a father saying that to a young Marine who had given so much to his country in a war? It is no wonder that there is so much hatred in the world. It is passed down from family to family, generation to generation, and no one seems to stop and think about it. They just accept everything as the truth without thought.

Years later Kate told me that the Flowers were relatives of the Goldwaters of Arizona and that Barry was named after the Senator. They must have known that the Goldwater family had Jewish blood running through their veins and yet they carried and passed on all of the hatred of generations. What would Preston, Barry's father, have done had he known that Barry's adopted son was not only Jewish but Catholic too?

Our son was born on April 1, 1946 in San Diego. I have enclosed a copy of the birth certificate for you. The doctor told me the original was destroyed and a new one naming Barry as the father replaced it but he did give me a copy of the original. I had him in my arms only a few hours but I loved him with all my heart, and much of my life since has been lived with sadness. If only I had been able to see you, talk to you. They named him Adam.

I have followed your career, Samuel. I read your book **Memories of War** and saw you on **60 Minutes** with Mike Wallace. I know about your family and how proud you are of them and how grand it is to hear you say that you have been married for 60 years. I saw Adam once when he played tennis in Burlingame, California. He reminded me of how I remembered you, so young and handsome. Your son Mark was there too, but I did not want to meet him.

Those few moments of bliss that we had has sustained me all my life and I am grateful that they were with you. I am not afraid to die nor do I regret my life. I do regret some of what Adam stands for and wonder if he knew the truth would he have taken the path he chose? I wonder, too, if Barry had not been so hard a taskmaster if Adam would have become so dogmatic and unbending in his belief in Jesus and Christianity being the only route for salvation. Kate told me that Barry was not the same man after he came home from the war. He drank heavily and was very bitter about his wounds. I guess many veterans felt that way.

Kate wrote me every month with news about Adam. I kept those letters in a box under my bed and read them repeatedly as the years went by. I had so many that I bought a computer and rewrote them onto a disc, the printout is attached.

The letters stopped coming in 1967. I was frantic and after 4 months, I called Kate's house in Austin, something I had promised myself I would never do. I asked for Kate and was put on hold. The young man's voice said, "This is Adam." I gasped for breath and told him this is Patricia Meisenger, a distant cousin of your mother. "You must be distant," he answered, "I never heard of you. She's dead, died 4 months ago." His voice was so cold, heartless that I could not talk; my hands were shaking so much I had to put the phone down. I do not remember how much time passed, but when I picked it up the dial tone was beeping. I made it to my room and I think I fainted. When I came to, I had to speak to someone so I called our priest, Father Carmody, and asked if he could hear my confession. I told him the whole story and for the first time since Adam's birth felt like a burden had been lifted. Now someone besides Kate and Barry knew. I told Father Peter that I had to have a way of knowing about Adam and he told me not to worry, he would take care of it and help me keep my secret. He did, too, his notes are also on the disc.

About five years later, I had built a wonderful relationship with Father Peter; he told me he was leaving the priesthood. His reasons were, for him, simple and concrete, his principles regarding religion and politics. His father, General Carmody, was involved in making decisions regarding the conduct of the war in Vietnam. As a military man, he followed the dictates of his President with no regard for his own personal feelings. That was his job. Father Peter was opposed to the war, the indiscriminate bombings of innocent people, the reasons we were told we were there, and he had a very long record of supporting the opposition in silence. After a confrontation with his father, he knew he could not be silent any longer and that meant he could no longer remain a priest. He told me that he would fulfill his promise to keep me informed about Adam and he did.

Dear Samuel when he found out that I was so ill he came to see me and told me that he knew you and your family well. I learned about his friendship with Mark and how close they were. He was very fond of you, Lillian, and your family. He had kept that to himself for so many years, never once hinting that he even knew you. He introduced me to an attorney who helped with my will. I also gave Mr. Giannini this letter to mail to you after....I was gone. How strange the workings of God that we should have such a connection.

Even now, we are still at war, still having so many young soldiers dying and suffering the effects of combat I am almost glad that my time on Earth is ending and that I will not have to read about the terrible ills that man brings to the world.

I do not know what you will do about this letter, Samuel. I do not even know if you will ever see it. If you do read it and decide to share it with your family or even with Adam I would like you to tell them I have, in one short encounter with you, fulfilled my being as a woman and that fulfillment has sustained me all of my life.

Goodbye and thank you

Pat Meisenger
June 10

After Mark read the letter, he had a difficult time deciding what to do. It was so powerful, so touching and possibly so devastating to all concerned that he even thought of destroying it. Days later, and from his memory of that day he told his three brothers, Alan, Jay, and Lee, "I was stunned by the contents of the letter. Learning that Adam Flowers was our half brother was devastating, a Christian Republican was hard to accept. Equally astounding was learning that Peter Carmody was involved. Peter was a learned writer very much in the news from time to time. I had spoken to him a few times over the years. When a new book of his came out or an editorial he had written became national news, I would call and congratulate him. Our youthful friendship did not go beyond that since we were too busy living our own lives. But now our lives would be intertwined, I needed his help and his advice so I picked up the phone and called."

"Mark, I have been waiting for your call, how good to hear your voice again."

"How did you know I would call, Peter?"

"I introduced Pat Meisenger to Antonio and we discussed it several times and decided you should receive the letter, not your father."

"Antonio?"

"Antonio Giannini, Pat's attorney."

"Oh. Peter, this letter, we need to talk. Can we meet somewhere?"

"Sure, it will be good to see you. Where and when?"

"New York, Boston, you tell me."

"I'll come down to New York, Mark. Get me a room, will you please?"

"No need for a room, friend, we can stay together in my parents' apartment."

Part One

Chapter One

Mark Davidson became acquainted with the impact religion has on politics in the election of 1960. Jack Kennedy was running against Richard Nixon and Kennedy's Catholic upbringing was getting a lot of press. Mark was 13 at the time, living in New Shrewsbury, New Jersey, and preparing for his Bar Mitzvah with Rabbi Arnold Ross at Temple Beth Shalom. His father Samuel, a lawyer and local judge, was not a religious man, but he insisted that all four of his sons attend Hebrew school and become Bar Mitzvah as well as attend Sunday school. Samuel, Lillian, his wife of 16 years and their two oldest children, Alan and Mark, regularly attended Friday night services. At a service in October 1960,

Rabbi Ross announced that his sermon the next week would be "Can a Jew Vote for a Catholic to become the President of the United States?"

Samuel gasped as soon as the Rabbi's words were spoken, "No, he can't do that."

"Why not, Samuel?" Lillian whispered.

"It is not a subject only Jews should hear, Lillian. The Rabbi has to share his opinions with the entire community. I must ask him to reconsider."

When the services ended and the receiving line was empty Samuel approached Rabbi Ross with extended hand and spoke to him in a gentle voice, "Lovely sermon tonight, Rabbi, as usual."

Rabbi Ross smiled, took Samuel's hand in his and said, "You say that every week, Samuel, and then you either add your opinion or ask me to do something. Do you have something on your mind tonight, too?"

"As a matter of fact, I do. About your sermon next week, Arnold, I think you need to make it in front of the clergy and leaders of our community, not just to our congregation. I would like you to consider postponing it for three weeks, give me a chance to contact the newspapers, get some publicity and speak to a few of my friends."

"But you don't know what I will say, Samuel."

"Don't need to know, Arnold. If religion is going to

become the determining factor in our elections, it is an American issue, not a Jewish issue. I for one will listen intently to whatever you say and I would expect the entire community has a stake in your thoughts too."

Rabbi Ross nodded in agreement as Samuel spoke and replied, "You have your three weeks, Samuel."

Chapter Two

The Red Bank *Register* published a long article about the coming Friday night service and the title of the Rabbi's sermon. Samuel played golf every weekend with General James Carmody, the commanding general of Fort Monmouth. General Carmody personally committed to come to the Friday night service with his staff and was very helpful in contacting the churches in the area with an invitation for their leaders and parishioners to attend.

The main chapel at Temple Beth Shalom had room for 400 people. The reception hall opened to the chapel and could hold another 300. The expectation was that a few hundred people from town would attend along with the 100 or so regular Friday night service attendees. The service always began at 7 PM, by 6:30 there were 800 people seated and standing with more arriving every minute.

Samuel and Lillian positioned themselves at the entrance to the sanctuary at 6:30. They made sure that General Carmody and his staff was seated in the front rows along with all of the visiting clergymen. Everyone was surprised to see so many people, especially the Catholic priests and other men dressed in robes. Catholics were forbidden to attend other churches and synagogues in particular. Perhaps that was so, but on this night, the subject matter overrode all restrictions.

The Red Bank *Register* reporter made an interesting observation in the article he wrote for Saturday's paper. "I looked around at the guests as the Friday night services were conducted before the Rabbi's sermon," he wrote. "Some of the lay people, the Mayor, and other dignitaries followed the services in the prayer book as best they could, but I did not see any of the Clergy participating."

When the first part of the service ended and the Rabbi approached the bema to begin his sermon, stillness descended on the room. Rabbi Ross adjusted the microphone and, without notes, began speaking. His voice resonated with passion.

"I know that this is not the season of the high holidays, that season passed a month or so ago. I am quite astounded at the size of the congregation tonight. I must thank all of you for coming. I do hope that I will be able to speak to you again in the coming weeks and months. In particular, I want to thank my fellow clergymen, General Carmody, and the elected officials that I see here tonight. When Mr. Davidson approached me about this, I thought it a good idea. Had I known that you thought it so important I might not have agreed to his proposal.

"It was only 15 years ago that we found out about the horrors inflicted on so many innocent people in the countries of Europe. It has saddened me that so little was done by the clergy to help prevent so many deaths, especially the Catholic leaders in Italy, Germany, Poland, and Czechoslovakia. There is no doubt in my mind that my brethren could have done much to help and that many Jews across America feel the same as I do. Now in 1960, we are being asked to vote for a young Catholic politician to become the President of the United States.

"The press and many Christian leaders as well as lay people have questioned John Fitzgerald Kennedy's willingness and/or his ability to separate his persona from the influence of the Holy See, the Pope in the Vatican. Where will his loyalty be when questions of faith arise, as they surely will? Will he be able to make decisions that affect the entire Nation, not just the Catholic population? I have examined this question for many, many months now and have reached this conclusion. If we cannot support any person of goodwill regardless of his personal beliefs, religious or otherwise, we will not find men of passion or good will to fill the elected offices in our country.

"We all know that those who choose to serve need religious and spiritual guidance. It has, and is important to all who serve us now, and in the capacity of leadership in the future. There is no doubt in my mind that Mr. Kennedy will, if elected, fulfill his obligation to the constitution and the nation. He, and others like him, know where their loyalties lie and those loyalties do not go out as public gestures but remain as private beliefs and concerns. If we examine the other contestant in the coming Presidential race, Richard Milhous Nixon, and only look at his heritage and religious belief, we must question his loyalty to his Quaker upbringing, and wonder if he could serve our Nation in time of peril and send our troops to war if it became necessary.

"Therefore, it becomes a moot question when we look at the religious background of these two candidates. We as Jews have the right to vote for either one depending only on our belief that one is better suited and will do a better job on behalf of the nation. Moreover, I might add, it bothers me to think of voters being lumped into categories by faith, race, color, region, ethnicity, and culture. We are a great nation because we are Americans all. Please turn to page 134 as we say the prayers welcoming the Sabbath."

Chapter Three

The Davidson family stood next to rabbi Ross as the guests left the Temple that night. Many regulars were effusive in their praise of the rabbi's talk and congratulated him. Some were overwhelmed by the context of his speech. General Carmody in particular made a point of congratulating his friend Samuel for making the evening possible and invited the rabbi to speak at his church as soon as he could arrange a date.

"We need to shift the thought process of exclusivity of paths to heaven to include every man," he said, "and that can only be done when we have dialogue with each other." That evening captured Mark's imagination and kept him from falling asleep nights thinking how wonderful it would be to have the knowledge and be able to influence people as Rabbi Ross had done. From that day on, he took his studies of Torah and Talmud more seriously.

In passing, General Carmody invited Mark to play tennis with his son Peter the next day at the courts at Fort

Monmouth. Samuel, as an ex- member of the military, was a member of the Fort Monmouth Golf Club and played there regularly. Mark did not like golf; it was too demanding competing with his father who carried a two handicap, so he had taken up tennis. Athletics was always a part of Mark's youth, little league baseball and football in season, but soon tennis became his only sport.

Mark met the General's son Peter the next day and they had a good morning on the court. After an hour of just hitting and fooling around, General Carmody and Peter played doubles against Colonel Matthew Foster, the General's aide, and Mark. The two young tennis players played a much better game than the adults did and both thought it incredible that the adults did not seem to mind. They had a lot of fun. Russ Cochran, the club tennis professional, watched them play and when they were finished, he asked Peter and Mark if they would like to take some lessons from him. When asked how much it would cost, he said it would not cost anything but their time and a commitment.

That was the beginning of a career as tennis players for the two boys and a lasting friendship began. With lessons every week from Mr. Cochran, Peter and Mark became a formidable doubles team and the next spring entered 12 year and under tournaments around the Monmouth County.

They each played singles with little success, usually losing in the early rounds, but they won several doubles events as partners.

It seemed that they played better as a team than as individuals and as the summer progressed, their rank rose to number 3 in the state. In the state championship, they reached the semis before losing to the number one seeds. As they started to grow taller and stronger, they began playing in the 14 and under and won the New Jersey State doubles championship. Both Peter and Mark advanced to the semi-finals in singles before losing. Their ranking of number one in doubles gained them entry to the National 14 and under Championship in St. Petersburg, Florida. It was there that Mark first met Adam Flowers of Texas.

Chapter Four

Adam was the number one junior player in the country in the 14-16 age division. He had won the Nationals at the age of 12 and was the number one seed in singles and doubles at St. Petersburg.

"You cannot imagine how important sports are, to kids our age, and Peter and I are no exception," Mark told a reporter. Both of them were on the Davis Racquet Company free list and had ample racquets and string provided at the beginning of the tennis season. Even though Peter and Mark's fathers could afford to buy their racquets, it was a sign of recognition when good young players were contacted by the better manufacturers, placed on a free list and used their equipment. Everyone wanted to be on the Dunlap free list because that was the racquet used by Rod Laver, the absolute best player in the world then and, arguably, the best player that ever lived. Adam Flowers was on that list. All the young players were impressed until they had a chance to get to know him on the tennis court and off.

There was no question that he was a polished player.

Adam lived in a huge house with a private court, trainer, and coach. Adam's family was very rich, Texas oil rich, and he let everyone know it. In a conversation with Peter one evening before they played against Adam and his partner, Mark said, "Do you see the way he struts around like a rooster without a care in the world?" From that day on Mark never trusted or liked anyone who walked that way, always suspicious of people who strut.

Adam was always dressed as if he was playing on center court at Wimbledon. Nevertheless, he could play and won the singles title easily. Peter was in his draw and got soundly trounced love and love. Peter was disconsolate but Mark told him, "We will get back at him in the doubles."

On the bus to the court to play the finals the next day, Adam walked up to Peter and Mark's seats, stared at Mark, and sneered, "What are you?"

Mark started to answer but Peter kicked him in the ankle and Mark just stared at Adam. Mark really did not know what the question was referring to either. As they walked to the court to warm up he asked Peter what Adam wanted to find out.

"Your religion," Peter answered, "but he already knew."

"Did you tell him?" Mark asked.

"Didn't have to, when he saw you in the shower he asked me how I could play with a Jew as a partner."

Mark and Peter won the first set and then it began to get

nasty. Adam was not used to losing so he started to call in balls out and when they crossed over, he began whispering "Jew boy" to Mark.

After the tournament, Mark told his father about Adam.

"At first I ignored it, but after 2 or 3 times I got really upset and that was when we lost the match. Peter tried to calm me down but I had lost it. I felt sorry for Peter but I was really angry at Adam Flowers for his unsportsmanlike conduct and his obvious delight in getting to me with his remarks."

"You will have to live with the fact that you are Jewish all of your life, Mark," his father said. "You have choices as to how you can react to what other people do or say. You can let it bother you and not say anything, you can say how you feel to those ignorant enough to make an issue of it, thereby letting them know that it bothers you, you can hide from it, or you can let it stimulate you to perform everything you do at the highest level. Should you choose the latter, eventually you will be judged by what you do, not by what religion you were born into or practice."

That evening Samuel called his two oldest sons Alan and Mark into his study. "I had an experience when I was your age that affected me deeply. I would like to tell you about it now."

Samuel had never told his children about his past, his youth. They knew he was a fighter pilot during the war and flew P-51's, but never heard any war stories. Samuel was close-mouthed about the cases he presided over and other than small talk about his youth and college, never revealed much about himself or his parents. This is what he told them.

In 1938, my family moved to a duplex house on Bond Street in Hillside, New Jersey. We were the only Jewish family in the neighborhood. Nineteen thirty seven was also the beginning of massive changes taking place in Germany. Hitler was on the march and the swastika, the Nazi symbol, was evident in nearly every picture from Germany. The German-American Bund, Germans living in America who supported all of Hitler's ideas about a super race and hatred of Jews, was prevalent in Hillside. In the neighboring town of Irvington, they displayed the swastika proudly in store windows and in front of their homes. Anti-Jewish rhetoric was printed and distributed on leaflets in our neighborhood and left on our doorstep.

One morning I walked outside and found that the entire side of our house had been painted with black swastikas. The fact that a Jewish family had moved into "their" neighborhood was unsettling to some of our neighbors and, eventually, to my family. Until that morning, I did not know that I was "different" but I soon learned that being Jewish in a Christian neighborhood had its challenges. My sister Maxine, who we called Micki, came home crying one day. "Who is Christ and when did I kill him?" she sobbed. Micki was only five and was friendly with an Italian girl, Mary who lived four houses away. It was five-year-old Mary, who asked Micki that question, but I doubt that it was she who posed it; it must have come from her parents or her older brothers, or worse yet, from her church.

Soon the invitations to the Ferrigno home and my walking to school with Mary's brother Ted stopped. Other young friends who lived on Bond Street stopped walking with me too. I imagined that their religion (they were Catholic) had a lot to do with my being excluded from their home and from my friendship with them. The Bond Street boys formed a team every sports season, baseball in the spring, football in the fall, basketball all year 'round. We played against other streets. After the swastika incident, I was no longer a part of the street team or included in the pickup games on the corner lot.

Neither of my parents was religious. Therefore, because my parents were not practicing Jews, my knowledge of Jewish culture, customs, and traditions was very limited. My mother wanted me to be Bar Mitzvah so I attended an orthodox synagogue for six weeks in order to learn enough Hebrew to read from the Torah. I hated it. I could not stand the Rabbi who was teaching me and I did not understand what I was learning because it was all in Hebrew. Somehow, I muddled through, and on a Saturday morning, I was called to the pulpit at the front of the synagogue to read the Torah and was deemed a man, as was the custom.

I did not attend services afterwards because my father, even when he was home, never attended. We did not have much money then either, it was the middle of the Depression. The Jewish kids in my school always went on the holidays but I stayed away. I became a loner, never really sharing my thoughts or my dreams with anyone, not even my mother. My father was a traveling salesman and only came home once or twice a month. I often wondered what it would be like to be a part of a group, to see my father every night, to have him share his experiences with me, to have a mentor. I was a very lonely young man who covered up that feeling by trying to be the best at whatever I was doing. In high school, I became a cheerleader and the manager of the basketball team. However, I did not have one "best" friend.

I was taking classes that would help me get into medical school. Latin and the sciences were necessary to take the college entrance exams. It took me four years to pass two years of Latin, and I dropped out of the chemistry class early on, as I had decided that I would not like to be a doctor after all. These decisions were mine alone. I had no counseling from my mother or the teachers in school. I graduated from high school in June, 1941. I had a scholarship to Rider College but no money for housing or food so I postponed entrance for six months. I worked at Crucible Steel to accumulate enough money to tide me over. Then, on December 7, Pearl Harbor was bombed and we went to war.

I enlisted in the Army Air Corps on my 18th birthday, took and passed the test to become an aviation cadet, wanting to become a fighter pilot. I received my wings in August, 1943. I suppose my independent nature and athletic skills made me want to fly fighter planes; I never wanted to fly bombers or transports. I was the only Jewish pilot in the squadron and only felt comfortable when we were flying, rarely when we were on the ground. I did not drink and drinking seemed to be a big part of a pilot's life. I knew I was accepted as a flyer but wondered if I was accepted as a Jew. In the air as a flight leader, I made instantaneous decisions that affected my life and many others' lives. They were life and death decisions.

That pattern of decision-making is still a part of my life. I rarely seek counsel. Making decisions without counsel or advice is not always the sensible approach when other people are involved. That your mother has had to put up with some of my decisions about our life without her input has been painful for her, I know. However, it has made me a better judge than some on the bench and that is almost as important to me as my family. I am doing exactly what I enjoy most, practicing law, and sitting on the bench judging cases in the context of the law.

Therefore, boys, I have some fatherly advice regarding who and what you are. You will always be Jews regardless of whether you follow Judaism as a religion, a spiritual calling, or a guide to personal conduct. True happiness comes from something to do, someone to love and something to look forward to. If you can find a profession, a job that you have a passion for, something to do that makes you eager to get out of bed in the morning and a loving wife, your life will be complete.

Mark started to say something when Samuel finished talking but Alan blurted out, "What about the war? Is that all you are going to say?"

"For now that is all I can say, wars are fought when one country attacks, invades or provokes another and then the young men of each nation kill and kill and kill until one country says stop. I lived through the war but so many that I knew did not. I have not talked about my experiences to Mom, my parents, Aunt Micki, anyone. I just cannot. I have not even come to terms with it myself, why I lived and so many died but I can talk about what prompted this discussion, and I will.

You will run into Adam Flowers types often and you will know them. You will also meet and interact with some men like Adam Flowers who befriend you, enjoy your company, and pretend to be your friend. Those you will not know until they reveal themselves. You will also interact with many genuine, caring, and worthwhile people of all persuasions. You may also notice that you and they are most comfortable among your own kind. And that is a pity because all of Humanity is equal in the eyes of Nature and Natural Law."

Chapter Five

Mark counted his youth in terms of age divisions in tennis, fourteens, sixteens, and eighteens. He played two years in each division. Peter and Mark remained doubles partners and touring juniors until Peter moved away when they were both 17. As partners, they won some matches and tournaments in different areas of the country. Mark played Adam Flowers 10 or 12 times, won some and lost some and never once enjoyed the experience. He played others and, whether winning or losing, always enjoyed the competition, challenges, and sportsmanship. In his senior year of high school, Mark won the state championship in singles and doubles. The last summer before he entered college, the last year of junior tennis was his best year of all. He won a number of tournaments on hard courts, clay, and grass. Mark played in so many venues and even competed in some men's tournaments against college players.

The absence of Adam Flowers in American junior tennis that summer also added to his enjoyment. Adam and his family were touring Europe and Adam had entered the junior sections of the French Open and Wimbledon. He played exceptionally well in both, reaching the finals of the French on clay and winning Wimbledon on grass.

Mark had a car that summer and spent much of his time seeing the sights, thinking about college and his future. He had enrolled in the school of arts and sciences taking his major in religious thought, and intended to become a rabbi. He did not enjoy playing doubles without his partner Peter. The depth of their friendship meant a lot to him.

Peter had attended several schools before coming to New Jersey. After they met, Mark became his only real friend. Their relationship was special, enhanced by the tennis partnership. Each of them knew what the other would do on the court and their competitive spirit carried them through many matches they should have lost. They were not as talented as many they played against but they won because of the closeness and that hidden instinct that came with their relationship.

Mark was a searcher, wanting to know why humanity had divided itself into so many hateful relationships. "With knowledge, he said, I could influence the world and make it into a better place."

He lost touch with Peter just before his first year started at Penn. Peter's father was transferred so Peter and the family moved with him. They said goodbye casually, not knowing they would not see each other again for nearly thirty years.

Academic life and athletics provided Mark with a great deal of fun and pleasure. Penn's tennis program was ideal in terms of competition and travel. Penn played against Ivy League teams, both military academies and selected universities from across the nation. Mark played number one in doubles with Paul Schwartz his roommate. He was number one in singles for four years and elected Captain his senior year. The only sour notes in his competitive career were the encounters with Adam Flowers. Adam was the number one player at the inter-scholastic series and league championships. Adam had grown more arrogant as his talent carried him to the number one ranking college player in the country. By reputation, he was a hard drinking, partying and very popular student in New Haven where he attended Yale University. There were many times when they played each other that Mark knew Adam had been drinking. "How bad am I going to beat you today, rabbi?" was his usual greeting when Penn played against his team

Years later, when he was telling Peter about Adam, Mark said, "He beat me more often than not but I never saw him so enraged as when I beat him in straight sets for the NCAA title. Then, after I was selected the number one player on the

All NCAA Team, he was furious. At the awards banquet he came to our table and in a loud and uncontrolled voice he shouted, 'You fucking Jews, always have to be better than everyone else, don't you!' His teammates had to pull him away to keep him from swinging the beer bottle he held at my head. 'Don't worry, rabbi," he shouted as he was led back to his table, "you and your Jew Boy friends will get it from me someday.'

Chapter Six

Adam Flowers came to international prominence in 1992. He had been a state senator in Texas since 1978 but resigned in 1988 to run for the United States Senate. The Flowers family used a lot of their financial power to help the Republican Party. This in turn gave them access to the White House and to the power the Republicans still have.

At age 28, Adam had been a hard driving oilman renowned for his lavish life style and long absences from Texas. His life changed dramatically when he drove a car off a bridge in Nassau, killing his best friend and two young girls. Adam was arrested by the police for drunken driving and charged with the killing of his three companions. It took the power of the American president to secure his release and his return to the United States, but only after a huge payment to Bahamian officials and a promise to his father of reform. He spent a year in the Betty Ford Clinic in Palm Springs and rediscovered religion and Jesus Christ.

He returned to Texas in the spring of 1974, a dedicated

born-again Christian with a passion to tell his story of redemption and work for promoting his newfound passion to Texans. His newly found principles added to his charisma and personality, and that appealed to the population in his wealthy district in Austin. He had been dating a young schoolteacher, Susan Forester, for years. She had rejected every proposal of marriage except the one he made when he returned home from the clinic. Their first child was a son, Matthew, born in 1975 and a daughter, Constance, was born a year later. Matthew became an all around athlete in high school and made Adam a very proud father. Constance was a brilliant student and a well- rounded, beautiful young woman: an actor, pianist, and painter. She was a National Merit Scholar her last two years in high school. Even though her mother, Susan, adored her daughter, Connie had no respect or admiration for her mother. Her father frightened her and the two of them never got along.

The Flowers family house was large and well appointed. Both Matthew and Connie had separate suites on the second floor. Susan and Adam had separate bedrooms on either side of a large, comfortable sitting room library filled with books, pictures, a wall sized television and audio equipment. Susan kept a well equipped bar hidden from view in a walk-in closet next to her bathroom.

Adam's political life began with a run for the Texas state

Senate in 1978. His election was easy, almost as if there had been no opposition. Then he cemented his popularity with forceful stands in opposing legislation that would legalize abortion, clean up the pollution along the Mexican border, and eliminate the death penalty in Texas. He led a committee that renounced the Federal ban on school prayer and insisted on States rights, namely the rights of Texans to permit prayers at all school functions. At Friday night high school football games, where his son played, he often led the prayers himself always ending with thanks to "My hero, the Lord Jesus," heedless of the fact that many of the attendees were not followers of his hero.

Chapter Seven

Adam never lost an election and, in winning a seat in the United States Senate, he became a power broker in Washington. Even though Adam was a freshman Senator, his powerful connections led to his appointment to the council of Foreign Relations and a place on the sub-committee investigating the BNL loan that the Atlanta branch of the large Italian government-owned Banca Nazionale del Lavoro had given to a foreign country. Former employees of the Atlanta branch of BNL approved over $3 billion in supposedly unauthorized loans to Iraq over the latter half of 1980 in this sensational case. These loans were never revealed to American and Italian banking officials.

When hearings began in 1990, Samuel was a judge in Atlanta where the case was tried. After the first day in court, he called Mark to ask, "Is this the same Adam Flowers you played against?"

"Must be, Dad, from the pictures I have seen he looks like the same guy. Why don't you ask him when he comes to court?"

A few weeks later Samuel called Mark again, "Was he always so arrogant, Mark?" he asked. "I never met a guy so sure of himself."

"That's the Adam I knew, Dad. He is shrewd and usually gets what he wants. At least he did when I knew him."

Mark had not seen Adam or thought much about him since he graduated rabbinical school in 1972 at the age of twenty-six. There were several job opportunities available, small congregations in small cities and towns but they did not appeal to him, so he decided to call Rabbi Ross and see if he would help him make a decision.

Mark met with Rabbi Ross at his synagogue in Oceanside, Long Island, where the rabbi had served since he left Red Bank. Congregation Beth Israel was a prestigious assignment in the Metropolitan New York area. Rabbi Ross was known as a deep thinking scholar with an aptitude for precise, succinct sermons and essays.

Rabbi Ross was genuinely glad to see Mark. He fondly remarked about how attentive Mark had been as a young man in his classes in Red Bank. "Always the student and seeker, Mark, I enjoyed watching you grow. That you are seeking wisdom from an older man flatters me and I hope I can help."

"My admiration for you has never wavered, Rabbi, and I

do need a job."

"You sound like I did 45 years ago, yes, just like all of my colleagues sounded when they first looked around and wondered who they were and how did they get where they were."

He said this in good humor, with a twinkle in his eyes and a laugh in his voice. "All you have to know is this, Mark: you know more than your congregants about your commitment to God and Judaism. If you are committed, and I think you must be, that knowledge will sustain you now and forever. Your father and I were discussing his life not too long ago. He told me that he has not been able to find a reason that he lived through the war and so many of his friends died. That question started me thinking, why have the Jews survived when so many have tried for so long to obliterate us? We are Gods' first born, Mark, we are here to show the light of goodness in mankind."

Mark knew then that he had made the right decisions, becoming a Rabbi and seeking the wisdom of Rabbi Ross. He accepted a position in a congregation in Rockville Center, New York.

Chapter Eight

Mark met Peter in the shuttle terminal at LaGuardia. They started to play "catch up" as soon as they got into the car.

"I wasn't so sure that I made the right decision when I left the states before I started college, Mark. It was not until I went to check out Oxford with my Dad that I knew I had made the right choice. I loved school but missed you and the athletic challenges of inter-scholastic competition."

"Why didn't you write?" Mark asked

"My father used to tell me that when he was in WW 2, as a young man, he would meet guys, become buddies, then be reassigned and never ever look back. Instant friends and instantly forgotten. It was better not to get too attached, he said. In combat guys are killed and being too close destroys your ability to carry on. We moved a lot when I was younger and I kept making best friends only to lose them. I guess his philosophy rubbed off on me, but who cares? Here we are now, in the present and that's all that counts."

"It really is good to hear your voice, Peter. What did you do after you left the States?"

"I went to Oxford for a year then enrolled at Georgetown in DC with a major in religious thought. Played some tennis when I got there, then quit. I wanted to spend my summers touring Europe and working. I worked for a year as a guide for American tourists then a year just taking Jewish students from all over the world to the death camps in Poland. That was the hardest task I had ever faced. After every trip I studied more, asked myself more, how did this happen? I wanted knowledge, Mark, knowledge that would give me answers.

"Living in Germany amongst those who lived through the war, some who objected but most who knew and did nothing, led me to the Church. The intensity of the training was inspiring; the immersion into the history and actions of the church was disturbing. I had great faith in God; still do, more now than before and that will never change. Nevertheless, the actions of man or lack of action when needed within the hierarchy, actions, and inaction that led to so many people that were persecuted and killed over the millennium, was hard for me to comprehend. Then Vietnam, my father's role in that disaster haunted me so I left the priesthood after five years.

"I met Patricia Meisenger shortly after I was ordained.

Pat had married a Navy officer in 1947 in San Diego. He was a carrier pilot and was at sea most of the time. He fought in Korea and had a command in the Vietnam War. Her husband went missing over Vietnam and is still among the missing from that disaster. She was a beautiful woman, Mark, tall and shapely. She walked like an athlete. She ran the adoption agency for Catholic Charities in Seattle. Her intelligence and good humor were evident. No one knew the burden she lived with or that she had a son. She told me that she would never remarry, that her life was lonely but not empty. She really loved her daily contact with the children she cared for.

"When she told me her story in confession, I became attached to her in a protective, spiritual manner that demanded more of me than I knew I could give. Her cry for help in keeping in touch with Adam was heart rendering. Could I help her? I didn't really know. Getting and forwarding information about another person, a person in the public eye such as her son Adam was, presented a physical and moral problem to me that was daunting. Could I do that in good faith? Could I even accomplish anything? When I decided I should at least try, I employed a clipping service and received a weekly report on the public life of Adam Flowers. I edited it a bit and sent a letter to Pat every month for years.

"That simple solution helped Pat learn about Adam as he grew in stature and became a very popular public persona. It also gave her news of Adam's children. Matthew was at Texas University, the star quarterback of the football team, as popular in Austin as his father. Constance was in the news too; she was an outspoken opponent of America's involvement in the war in Iraq. Adam was very embarrassed by her stand and their feud was often in the headlines. As it became more vocal, they became more distant. The father daughter relationship ended when she converted to Judaism and married David Rothman, the heir to the Rothman real estate empire in New York. Neither Adam nor Susan attended the wedding. Adam publicly denounced her."

"Wait a minute, Peter, this is getting out of hand. Constance Rothman is Adam's daughter. The Rothmans belonged to my congregation; I gave instruction to Constance for a year before the wedding. I married Constance and David. I have not seen them since they moved to the city a few years ago but I consider them friends. Now she is my niece?"

"Go back far enough, Mark, and we are all related. That is what had troubled me most of my life. I met her at a book signing in 2000. The Rothmans had a small dinner party for me, David and Connie sat at my table. I told Constance that I knew her father when he was a very young man. She was cordial but cold, her reaction quite different from what I had expected. She had no way of knowing I was a former priest but I did not hesitate to say that our lives are enhanced by forgiveness.

She hesitated for several minutes, smiled a shy smile before she asked me what he was like when he was young.

Not very nice, I said and she roared with laughter. Tell me more, please tell me more.

"And I did. We became friends but I have never revealed more than that to her. I think she has a right to know everything now that her grandmother has passed away. We are invited to their home tomorrow night for dinner and I expect that we will discuss what you and I are doing together."

Chapter Nine

The Rothmans lived in a remodeled town house on East 63rd Street just off 5th Avenue only a few blocks from the Davidsons' apartment. Peter and Mark arrived at 6:30, rang the doorbell. Constance greeted them warmly with hugs for both and thanked them for coming.

"This is such a pleasure for me, Rabbi, Peter. That we all know each other is a fascinating revelation and an indication of the small world we live in."

"Smaller than you think, Connie," Peter answered as David came down the stairs into the hallway. After introductions, David escorted them into the dining room. When dinner was finished, they sat at the table over coffee for an hour. The conversation about Peter and Mark's friendship and their lives since ended when Peter started talking about Adam.

"When we first met three or four years ago, Connie, I told you that I knew your father. By the way, where is Sara?"

Sara was the Rothman's three-year-old daughter.

"David's parents have taken her to the shore for the weekend. She loves the beach."

"Connie," Peter continued, "When I was a parish priest I heard confession from one of my women parishioners. She told me about a relationship she had in 1945 with a young pilot on Iwo Jima. That relationship resulted in her pregnancy and the birth of a son in 1946. Her name was Pat Meisenger."

"My grandmother was a Meisenger, were they related?"

"Yes, they were first cousins. Connie you are related to her too, she was your real grandmother."

"That can't be, Peter, I would have known."

"It is true, Connie, and I am involved too," Mark echoed. "The young pilot was my father Samuel. That is why we are here tonight. I received a letter from an attorney in Seattle who forwarded a letter Pat had written just a few months before she passed away in June. It was supposed to be sent to my father. However, Peter and Antonio Giannini, her attorney, thought it best to send it to me. I have a copy for you if you want to read it."

Connie was sobbing, David put his arm around her, pulled her close, and handed her a tissue. "Does her father know, or Matthew?"

"We here in this room are the only people who know," Peter responded. He added that he and Mark did have a plan and then shared it with Connie and David.

"We have decided that Samuel should be told, that Mark should find a way to do it informally. Then, after he reads the letter, Mark should send a copy to his three brothers and the four of them, in conjunction with their Mom and Dad, should decide if they want to do anything about Adam, tell him, or not tell him. The conundrum is what we would want to accomplish by telling Adam. Mark has some ideas. I do, too, but it affects more than just the Davidsons' immediate family. You and Matthew have to be considered, Constance, we will not take the next step until you and David make a decision, first about yourselves, then after you have met with Matthew, if you decide to meet with him, that is. After that, it becomes more complicated. Who should tell Adam and under what circumstance?"

Every question, every answer, brought more questions. It was midnight before they all decided that they would meet for breakfast in the morning.

Chapter Ten

"Constance and I were up most of the night," David began, "we did an extra twenty minutes on the treadmill this morning to try and settle us down. It helped some but not much. We have so many questions."

"If we have the answers, you will have them," Peter said.

"First, does Adam know he was adopted?" Connie asked.

"Pat told me that Kate never told him. If Barry did, we do not know. I suspect not, but can't be sure." Peter responded.

"Why do you think he should know? Do you want to change him, drive him absolutely crazy, and expect him to accept this?" Connie whispered.

"Those are the 64,000 dollar questions, Connie," Mark responded. "Peter and I asked them, too. Yes, we do have a reason that he should know. He is a very powerful Senator, Constance. Adam Flowers believes in Christianity as a national religion. He will not stop working towards that end until it happens. He also believes that we live in the "End

Times," and, like millions of other fundamental Christians, he sees Rapture in the near future.

"We want to try to convince him that the path he is taking is wrong for humanity. Whether he would even listen to us is a challenge, gamble if you will. Neither of us can approach him. Matthew and you are the only people he might listen to."

"I haven't seen or spoken to my father in three years, Mark." Connie was crying softly as she spoke. "If Christians sat Shiva he would have done that for me and I would have been dead in his mind." She wiped her eyes as she spoke. "I am not sure Matthew would even agree to meet with me. I hardly know him now at all. Matthew is his father's son, has his passion for Christ, and works for the religious arm of the Republican Party."

Mark spoke in a gentle voice when he stated, "We thought that it might be helpful if someone other than you would contact Matthew and tell him you wanted to have a meeting with him."

"He'll ask why," Connie replied. "What will you tell him?"

Peter told her, "I could call Matthew, I was a priest, you know, and a friend of the family. I could tell him that you would like to try and reconcile with your father."

"I don't know. We were never close and I never

discussed David or my conversion with him."

"If you told Adam that you were expecting a baby and wanted them to be a family again would that have an impact on him?" Mark asked.

She shrugged her shoulders, looked down at her feet and said, "They don't even know I have a 3 year old daughter. Why do you think I will tell him I'm pregnant? "

"She is pregnant you know," David chimed in.

"The two of you must be psychic," Connie chuckled, "I'm still not sure I want to do this, Peter, Mark. I would feel better if I knew and believed in the reason you are pursuing this."

Peter walked over to where his brief case was resting, pulled out a paperback book, and handed it to Connie. "Please read this, Constance. It is long, scholarly, but very informative and contains hints of why we want to talk to Adam." He handed her a copy of James Carroll's book *Constantine's Sword*. "It may take you some time to read it. When you are finished, I am sure that you will be able to make a more informed decision about the path we would like you to take. When that happens I would appreciate your contacting Mark so he can give you our timetable and tell you of his progress with his father, Samuel. Also, please let us know if you made contact with Matthew and what his reaction to meeting you was or if I can do anything to help.

It was wonderful seeing you and David again, Connie. When is the baby due?"

"March, 6," David answered as he took Peter's hand. "It was a real pleasure being with both of you and I hope we can see each other again in the near future."

After he returned home, Mark received a letter from Peter indicating they had accomplished a lot in New York. It read, in part, "It was great reconnecting with you Mark, just great." Mark, of course, felt the same way. Peter also included a quote from a newsletter by Dr. James Dobson, President of *Focus on the Family*, a fundamental Christian organization and powerful friend of and fundraiser for the Republican Party.

Dear friends and contributors,

You should be heartened to know the impact you have had. If we can work together again this year, with your prayers and financial support, we can continue the good work that was so significantly begun last year. There is an opportunity for a new beginning in 2006. It is an opportunity that should not be wasted nor frittered away. I believe we can do things together that none of us could do alone. Your prayer and financial support for these organizations allows us to "be there," to take actions and speak out for important issues for families, and to open the door for people to hear about the life- saving message of Christ.

Let me say again two things that I have said repeatedly during this past election: First, without prayer and fasting by many, all of our other efforts would have been in vain. Second, as I continue to say, no matter how many ballot measures we pass, no matter how many constitutional amendments we support, no matter how many God-fearing and God-honoring women and men are elected and appointed to public office, until the hearts of the people change, we will not turn around this culture and restore our Biblical foundations. May we continue to pray collectively for this spirit of revival throughout America!

Peter wrote,

"Biblical foundations, Christianization of America. This man has power and exposure, Mark; he and others like him must be made to understand that some, like you and me, do not want this to happen. I will be changing my address soon and will let you know where you can reach me by mail and phone next week. Do you think we can have a hit the next time we see each other?"

Fondly,

Peter

Chapter Eleven

Mark cancelled his appointments, rearranged his schedule, then called his Dad and asked him if he wanted to go away for a few days, "Just the two of us on the golf course in Pinehurst, Dad. How does that sound to you?"

"You know how it sounds to me, Mark, and you also know how it will sound to your mother. You ask her, son, she always says yes to you."

The following week Mark flew down to Raleigh and met Samuel at the airport. He had not seen his father since his parents had moved to Florida six months before. Samuel was tan, very trim and without the beard that his family thought made him look so much older. "How you hitting them?" was a standard first question Mark asked whenever they had not seen each other for a while.

"Not playing too much these days, Mark. Handicap is 10 but from the white tees; cannot seem to get more than 200 yards with the driver and that makes it tough to play from farther back. And you?"

"Just hit some balls once in a while. Haven't been on a course since the last time we played at Old Orchard."

Samuel had been the club champion for eight years at Old Orchard in Eatontown, New Jersey. Mark caddied for his father whenever Samuel played a tournament there and learned a lot about life and golf from watching him play. Samuel played by the rules in everything he did and it taught Mark a strong lesson that he still lived by. Neither man found it difficult to speak freely about any subject so Samuel knew that Mark had an agenda besides the golf.

"Good to see you, son. You must have something on your mind though, you have not taken any time off since you joined the Council two years ago."

"You're on my mind, Dad, and I wanted to play Pinehurst especially after watching the Open a few weeks ago. Besides, we haven't talked much in the past few years and I needed a change of scenery."

"You really never have changed, Mark, always taking care of others without revealing much of yourself. I don't believe this get-together is about you."

Mark had not made up his mind yet about telling Samuel about the letter. He really wanted to see what his father's mental state was, feel him out about what he remembered about the war, if he wanted to, or could talk about his experiences. His father really was his best friend and he had to find the right avenue to walk him down a new path.

Samuel had had some frustrating and angry exchanges with Adam Flowers at Senate hearings in Washington and Atlanta. He told Mark more than once that he did not like the guy. "He's one stubborn SOB," he said on more than one occasion. "But I have to give him credit; he is loyal to his principles even if they are quite different from mine."

Pinehurst was an hour from the Raleigh Airport. They rode in silence. Samuel seemed preoccupied and Mark did not want to talk either. The attendant took their clubs and bags; they checked in and went to their rooms. It was 4:30 and dinner was not until seven.

"Let's go to the range, Dad," Mark suggested when he was finished unpacking and went to his father's room.

They walked down the path in front of their Villa, passed the statue of Payne Stewart, paused to reflect on his victory in the U.S. Open of 1999. Then Samuel just seemed to drift away. His shoulders drooped, his pace slowed and his voice was sad as he asked if it would be OK to pass on the range and just get a beer at the bar.

"Are you OK?" Mark asked.

"Never OK in the summer, Mark, less OK this year."

"Why?"

"Sixty years ago I was on Iwo Jima flying missions over Japan. Every day now, I see faces, hear voices, and remember friends. Today, July 8, its Al Sherren and Pudgy Carr, both killed. Al and I went all through flying school together. Pudgy and I shared a tent on Iwo. July 3rd it was Dick Schroeppel, June 1, Danny Mathis, today Sherren and Carr. I was on that mission too, Al called in "I'm hit, I can't see, and he was gone. Pudgy just never showed up when we rendezvoused for the return flight. As I get older I wonder more why I have had a life and they did not. Sixteen pilots I flew with did not come back. So I'm kinda hurting every day, son."

An image flashed in front of Mark's eyes: the letter Pat had written said today was the day she met Sam, had consoled him, and made love to him.' Could the subject be broached now? He decided not to, it was not the right moment; He would let his father talk as much as he wanted and wait for another opportunity.

They sat at a table overlooking a large lake, ordered beer and a snack. When the waiter placed their order on the table Samuel raised his glass, said 'Kampai,' nodded his head toward Mark and drained his glass. How ironic Mark thought, Kampai, Japanese for Cheers, Bottoms Up, and L'Chaim. Samuel, who had hated the Japanese so much, now uses that drinking phrase almost exclusively.

Mark always admired his father for his courage, tenacity, and flexibility. Samuel had gone to Japan for a legal conference in October, 1983. When the Davidson family gathered for Thanksgiving that year, Samuel was effusive in his remarks before he cut the turkey.

"I never had a desire to visit Japan or get to know Japanese people, experience their culture. I went because your mother wanted to see gardens and buildings that she had seen photographs of and had admired for so long. I have to tell you it was an eye opening experience for me. What I witnessed was very different from my vision of Japan and her people. I only knew them from the war, when we were at war. I realize now that one should not form categorical opinions of anyone without having firsthand experiences with them."

As it happened, their youngest son, Lee, was close to graduation from college and Lillian thought that Lee would like Japan, so they gave him a trip for his graduation present.

Lee spent six weeks living with a family in Shizuoka Province in 1984 and decided to stay in Japan and teach English for one year. That year kept extending itself and Lee met and married a Japanese woman, the daughter of an officer in the Japanese Air Force in WW 2. The two fathers who would have killed each other when they were 21 met at the wedding of their children in March 1988. Now they had three grandchildren and the love that flows between the grandparents and the grandchildren know no boundaries of race, religion, or nationality. They had gone from enemy to family forty-three years after the end of the war. Mark recalled that story as he wondered what his Dad's reaction would be if or when he finds out that Adam Flowers is his son.

Chapter Twelve

The Number 2 course at Pinehurst hosted the 2010 U.S. Open. Both father and son wanted to play it, actually experience what they had both seen on T.V. They booked tee times for early the next morning. Their clubs and caddy were waiting for them at the practice range when they arrived at the first tee a few minutes before their starting time.

On the course, they were forced to play shots neither had ever used before, putting to the hump-backed greens with three woods, putters and chipping with wedges, 7 and 9 irons. Their scores were not too good but they each enjoyed the variety of experiences they shared on this difficult golf course. Mark thought it worth the $300.00 green fee and $60.00 for the caddy, but Samuel was horrified when he found out that Mark had spent almost $800.00 for a round of golf. "I could have bought 3 full sets of clubs for that amount of money in the 60's," was what he exclaimed.

Samuel was a lot more relaxed at dinner that night. Mark

wanted his father to talk about Iwo Jima without changing his demeanor so he asked, "Did you ever see Bob Hope on Iwo Jima, Dad?"

"Saw him and his entourage on Oahu in '44. Great show, Jerry Colona, Frances Langford. Hope was swinging a driver constantly while at the mike. They never got to Iwo but we did get a small troupe once, two guys and two girls. They were there on July 8 when we came back from that mission. I remember because it was the first time I did not take Benzedrine before reaching the target and I was exhausted. One of the girls, the accordionist, Pat Meisenger was her name, came up to me on the flight line after the show and we spent the entire night talking. I had not spoken to a girl for nearly two years, Mark. She reminded me of home, why I was fighting, of your mother, and what I could look forward to when I came home, if I came home. She made love to me."

Now, Mark thought, now. But how? "She's dead, you know."

Samuel was shocked, his eyes wide as he responded in a loud voice, "Dead? How the hell would you know that?

"I received a letter from her attorney in June. It was supposed to be sent to you, but Mr. Giannini sent it to me instead. I have a copy in the room and did not know if I should let you read it. That is why we came down here, Dad. I wanted to see how you were, assess your physical and mental condition. That is the Rabbi in me, I did not know what to do, and you gave me the opening I needed. It is a shocker, Dad, and I still do not know if I should give it to you. Your call, Dad, your call."

The waiter appeared with their dinner. Samuel, visibly upset said, "Not now, young man. Bring me a scotch and soda, make it a double, please, I will let you know when I want my food."

The waiter placed Mark's dinner in front of him and hurried away. Mark picked at his food in silence as Samuel watched for the waiter to return with his drink. "I cannot believe your timing, son, you could have at least waited until we finished dinner."

The waiter returned with Samuel's drink and Samuel fingered the glass before he took a sip and looked at Mark and said, "How long have you had it?"

"A month."

"Anyone else read it?"

"Yes, but I won't comment until you have read it, too."

"Give it to me in the morning, Mark. I want to try to get a good night's sleep before I read it." Samuel finished his drink, said good night to Mark, and left the dining room.

The next morning Samuel ordered breakfast from room service. He picked at the food as he read the letter for the first time. Struck by its content he paced the room, ordered more coffee, and read it again. It was lunchtime before he called Mark and told him he should eat alone. They had planned to eat lunch in the main dining room but when Samuel was finished reading the letter he asked his son to cancel the reservation. "I think I want to eat in my room, son. I don't know if I want to talk just now, Mark, perhaps it would be best if you ate by yourself."

Surprised by Samuel's reaction Mark went to his room, put on jogging shoes and went for a run around the golf course that fronted his building. He returned to his room at noon. He was never hungry after a good run, so he went to the breakfast bar for coffee and a snack. Samuel was sitting at a small table overlooking a fountain. He saw his son come in and motioned him to join him.

"Have a good run?' he asked.

"Gets rid of the tension and there is lots of that in today's world, especially here and now."

"I look that bad, eh?"

"Want to talk?"

"Sure. About what?...Just kidding. Funny we should be here on this day but 60 years later. Some letter, eh? Some life she had compared to mine. What should I do, Mark?" He said that with a sigh, not a question, not a statement, just a thought.

"I've had the letter for a month now," Mark said,

"thought of nothing else, night and day. The only positive from it was getting back in touch with Peter. You remember him, don't you, Dad?"

"Of course, but I never thought of him as a priest, did you?"

"That is another subject, let's stick to this one. I called Peter after I collected my thoughts and we met in New York to talk things over. Adam has two children, Matthew, about 30, and Constance, 28. She married a Jewish man four years ago, converted, and lives in New York with her husband, David, and three-year-old daughter, Sara. Neither of her parents was at the wedding. As you can imagine from Adam's very vocal statements, he was not happy with her choice of a husband. As she put it, 'If Christians sat *Shiva* I would be dead in my parents' eyes now.' We did not talk about it but I know she did not have an easy time with her life as a youngster.

"The letter blew her away as it did all of us. We really do not know what to do. I think Connie would just like to forget about the whole thing and move on with her life. Peter does not want that to happen. He gave her a book to read about the Church and Jews. He also sent her some excerpts from a James Dobson newsletter about the powerful political push for Christian ideals to lead our nation. A national religion, if you can believe that."

"Peter and I discussed this at length. Maybe, just maybe this will pique her interest and lead to having Connie and Matthew attend a meeting we are planning with our family on your anniversary next month. The boys don't know anything yet, and I won't tell them until you and I sort out about what, if anything, you want to do Dad."

"My first reaction was to forget it, let it go. Then I had a thought, he is a powerful person leading our nation down a path that I cannot live with. Maybe this new twist in his life will open his eyes and help change the direction he is going now. Then it would be worth a try. I'm not too hopeful, but don't you think we should make the effort?"

"My thoughts exactly, Dad; but first I have to find a way to reach him, meet me face to face, and that is a challenge."

Chapter Thirteen

The letters Kate had sent to Pat over the years set the theme of Adam's life. Kate's difficult existence with Barry became apparent from the first letter and remained constant throughout the years. Barry had been a fabulous, fun loving, handsome young man when they first met at Camp Pendleton in 1942. He told Kate that he had found a home in the Marines that gave him an entirely new perspective and purpose in his life. His father, Preston, had kept him isolated and within the strict confines of school, church and the family business, oil. Life had not been fun for him. His father had plied him with rewards for performance in all aspects of his life: A pony when he was eight and made the honor role for the first time, a horse when he won his first tennis championship, a convertible Chevy when he was 15 and led his high school debating team to a state title.

Against his father's wishes, Barry joined the Marines the day after he graduated high school. He wanted independence and thought the military would help him find himself. He flourished under the strict regime. His personal rewards for excellence were the recognition by his trainers that gave him promotions to leadership. First, he became a platoon leader, then the company sergeant and when he completed boot camp, he was asked to go to officers' training. He was a second lieutenant when Kate met and fell in love with him. They were married six weeks after they met. Barry shipped out in late 1942 for Hawaii; Kate took a job as a nurse's aide at the base hospital and lived with three other nurses in a small house in Oceanside. Letters from Barry came sporadically. She read about the invasions of Makin and Tarawa, and wondered where Barry was and if he was OK. It was a year before they were reunited in San Diego. Barry had been reassigned to the 5th Marines and reported for duty at Pendleton in January 1944.

They had six months together before he shipped out again. They wanted a baby but nothing happened even though they tried often.

It was difficult for Kate; letters did not arrive as she had planned. She lived in fear for seven months before she received a telegram from the war department. It read, "Captain Barry Flowers has been wounded on Iwo Jima and will be sent to the Naval Hospital in San Diego for treatment and recovery." She was at the pier when his hospital ship docked and she followed the ambulances to the hospital near Balboa Park. Kate paced the waiting room floor for a day before she was taken to his ward. Barry was awake, lying on a traction bed, doing pull ups when she first saw him. Kate fought hard to hold back the tears; Barry smiled weakly and reached for her hand. She bent down, kissed him, and started to cry.

Barry's left leg had been amputated above his knee and his internal wounds needed more surgery. He was in the hospital for three months before he was discharged from the hospital. Kate had rented a small house near the beach in Del Mar when Pat called about the baby and it was there that Adam lived for the first three years of his life. (Barry only walked on his prosthesis when he wore long pants.) Kate and Adam loved the beach; Barry never joined them but watched as they played in the sand and frolicked in the surf. Kate would look back and see him on the porch of their house, always a beer in hand, and wave. He just stared out to sea. In 1949, Preston Flowers died and left his fortune to Barry in the form of a trust. He had sold his business but kept his vast ranch and home in Austin. Barry wanted to return to Austin so they moved back to Texas and Adam started school.

The Flowers ranch had all sorts of sporting areas on the property: a baseball diamond, basketball court and a clay court for tennis. It was on the tennis court that Adam excelled. He spent hours hitting against a backboard, then more time hitting serves over the net. Barry watched him from a distance, then hired a pro and Adam won his first tournament at 12 in Dallas. When he came home there was a horse tied up in the back yard as a reward. Adam continued to grow, to win. Every achievement was rewarded, never with kind words or hugs, but with material things.

He was learning what Barry had learned from his father: the rewards for winning far exceed the satisfaction one receives for performing to your potential, be it in sports, business, or politics. Ingrained with this philosophy from childhood, Adam became obsessed with coming out on top in everything he attempted regardless of the tactics employed.

When he was fourteen, he paid the daughter of the stable master fifty dollars to have sex with him. Two weeks later, he felt a burning sensation when he urinated and sought out his father. Barry laughed at him and said, "You should have used a rubber." Humiliation by his father had not been expected. Confused and angry Adam sought out the local veterinarian who took him to a clinic in the next town where he received a shot of penicillin and advice from the doctor about future sexual encounters. Years later, after he had married Susan, he told her what happened and said, "I felt as if I was drowning in our back yard swimming pool and my father walked by and said, You should have learned how to swim when I told you to,' and then walked away. It hardened me, Susan, and I never trusted anyone fully ever since."

Barry began drinking more heavily as the years quickly disappeared. As time went on, he became more and more abusive to Kate and distanced from his son. Kate moved into another wing of their large house, always wanting to leave Barry but bound not to, afraid of what would happen to Adam.

When Adam was sixteen, he and Barry flew to Africa to go hunting. While there, he started to drink, first wine and beer with his Dad and then vodka by himself. After three weeks in Africa, they returned home and Adam felt the need to have alcohol every day in some form. Usually a beer or two would suffice but by the age of twenty, just after Kate died, he needed more. Just as Barry had needed to get away from his father, Adam needed to get away from Barry. When Adam graduated from Texas, he stayed in Austin and entered law school. When he passed the bar, he took a job with the firm in Austin that handled his father's trust and entered politics in 1978.

Peter Carmody had arranged for Pat to receive clippings and news stories about Adam's life and career from a clipping service. She received them weekly until she passed away in June. Every piece of information was included in the package that Mark had received from Mr. Giannini in June.

Chapter Fourteen

Mark called Peter shortly after he returned home from Pinehurst at the only number he had and was told that it had been disconnected so he wrote him an email. It was three days before he received an answer; "will call you in a day or so. Peter."

"Where have you been?" Mark asked when he picked up the phone.

"In Austin; spent the last four days with Matthew Flowers."

"And?"

"He is amenable, at least to speaking to Connie. He has not seen her since her wedding and had only spoken to her once or twice since. I think he is going to meet her in Chicago next week. Did you speak to your father, Mark?"

"I did, we were away for four days. I told him that is was up to him if he wanted to go any further. I pointed out why it might be important to the country and he agreed. What I would like to see happen is this: Connie and Matthew agree to fly down to Tampa to meet with my father and brothers. If there is agreement that Adam should be approached, we hack out a plan and put it into action. If that is successful and Adam will agree to meet Samuel, we arrange for the entire family to attend a celebration of my parent's 60th wedding anniversary on August 15, either in Florida or in Asheville. Cooler in the mountains but cheaper in Florida and they are near the beach. Details can be worked out as each step brings confirmation of the next. What do you think, Peter?"

"Sounds like a plan. Step one is Connie and Matthew and we will know soon. By the way, Mark, I will be moving to San Francisco in a few weeks. There is more, but that is enough for now. I will keep my email address and send you the phone number when I am settled. Connie is supposed to email me and copy you, when they make a decision. Ciao, friend." Two days later an email from Peter appeared on the screen. It read, "They will meet in Chicago over the weekend. Will stay in touch. Peter."

Chapter Fifteen

Connie met Matthew on July 24 in Chicago's Hilton Hotel on Michigan Avenue. Their rooms were on The Club floor and they met in the lounge on the top floor of the Hotel. Matthew was cordial but cold when he greeted his sister. "Hello, Connie, you are looking well. Been a while, hasn't it?"

"Only three years, not too long in time, Matthew, but the distance between us seems to have gotten bigger. Too bad, isn't it?"

"If you are going to start this conversation with the religious, political shit, I am going to say good bye right now."

"Can't help it Matthew, we just lost the 2200th soldier in your President's invasion of a foreign country." Matthew glowered at her as she added, "And then there is the place where your father is taking us."

"Can I have a drink?"

"Typical Flowers solution, stall for time with a high ball."

"You haven't changed much either, Sister." Matthew said angrily as they sat down on the small sofa. Connie poured a scotch and soda and handed it to her brother.

"How about one for you, Sis?" Matthew asked.

"Pregnant women don't drink, Matthew, but I stopped long ago."

"Great news, when?"

"March."

"How's David?"

"Same old, same old. Not too happy that I am here with you. Furious at what you are doing with the Republican Party."

"All I am doing is following in my father's footsteps. Is that why I am here, Sis?"

"No, Matthew, you are here because of this letter. It was given to me a week ago and I was asked to give it to you."

Connie handed Matthew the letter, hesitated a moment before she left him alone in the room. She needed to breathe some fresh air so she went for a stroll through the park and along the lakefront across Michigan Avenue from the hotel. When she returned to the club lounge, an hour or so later, Matthew was not there nor was he in his room. She called the front desk to inquire if he had checked out and they said no. She wondered where Matthew could be, what did he think, where is this all leading; she called room service and ordered a vegetable plate and tea. Connie finally called Matthew at eight that evening, "Have you eaten yet?" she asked. He told her no and they agreed to meet in the coffee shop. Connie saw him across the restaurant, menu in hand, sitting in a booth in the rear of the restaurant. He was wearing a sweat stained, hooded sweater, track pants and shoes and holding a towel to his wet face.

"Where did you go, Matthew? I was worried."

"Clearing my head, Sis. Haven't done 3 hours in years. What do you want to eat?"

"Eat? I want to talk. I can't eat, Matthew."

"This is about us, isn't it, Connie. Two children from the same father taking different paths that split the family irrevocably."

"Perhaps, in a small way, but it is so much more than that, Matthew. It's about how I feel about the world, past, present and future. What you and your father are doing with this Crusade you are leading to Christianize America. Where will that lead us, dear brother? All that this situation has done is put me in a place where I am questioning my very existence, my purpose in life and what will happen to my children."

Matthew ordered a roast beef sandwich and a Corona beer without revealing that he had heard anything that Connie had said. Then, looking her square in the eye, said,

"He's your father, too, Connie. I knew you were a thinker, Sister, but never thought you took things so seriously. What happened?"

"What happened, Matthew, is this;

I met a former priest and a rabbi who have concerns. They gave me the letter from Pat to read and a book to study and those two items have consumed me for a month. Every answer I come up with leads me to a hundred questions for which I have to find answers. Matthew, please finish your sandwich and, if you want to talk, call me. If I have the energy we can meet later, if not, it will have to wait until tomorrow." Exhausted, she got up and left.

It was midnight and she was pacing her room deep in thought, looking for answers to questions she knew that Matthew was going to ask her. Why had she converted to Judaism? She needed to hear herself say it, ponder it, and feel sure it was the truth. What had been a conversion of accommodation to David and his family took on new meaning after she read, reread, the marked passages in Constantine's Sword. As she read the pages she became Jewish, felt the fear and faced the torment of anti-Semitism; saw the large cross on the backs of the Crusaders as they plunged their swords into the enemies of Christ, the Jews, the Muslims. She rode the train to Auschwitz and smelled the stench of bodies rotting in the boxcar.

She reached deep into her jewelry box, pulled out the silk scarf that held Grandmother Kate's legacy close to her and fondled the gold cross Kate had worn all of her life. The cross symbol of Jesus, his murder, reminder that he died for our sins and she started to cry. This symbol of love from the past had now become a symbol of hatred, separation, and Christian superiority. Connie folded it back into the scarf and threw it into the trashcan.

A moment later, she retrieved it. "How could I throw away the memory of the grandmother whom I never knew, who had believed what she had been taught, lived in fear of punishment, of an afterlife in Hell if she did not follow the dictates of the Church on Earth. And now I have become convinced that what she read, what dictates she followed, did not come from Jesus or God but from man."

She pondered, thought, meditated, prayed, and cried a lot. If God lives in all that exists, then a human being may have no great need of the mediating institutions of church or synagogue to be in contact with the Divine. Similarly, a political society's main goal should be respect for every member as equal to every other, since all are instances of God's presence. The sovereign is to be valued no more than any citizen.

As she pondered these questions, she found the answer to why she was here meeting with Matthew.

The phone rang the next morning; she sat up, looked at the clock, and then picked up the phone. It was Matthew.

"Sis, its 9 o'clock, are you up?"

"Yes, up, up but not dressed. Give me an hour."

"I'm going for a run, see you in an hour. Lobby restaurant, OK?"

"No, my room, I'll have room service bring breakfast."

Chapter Sixteen

Matthew looked refreshed when he walked into Connie's room. He was still wearing his sweat suit, carried his sneakers, and had a sly grin on his face. He walked over to where Connie was standing, took her around, and kissed her flush on her mouth. She drew back. "What's that about, Matthew?"

"It's about me, Sis, and how I feel. Didn't know how dreary I was until this morning. The DC blues they call it in Washington, cabin fever. Being here and seeing you has given me some relief. What's for breakfast?" he asked as he took the lid off the plate on the table.

"Bacon and eggs over easy, you always liked them cooked that way."

"You got it right, for once," he said with a twinkle in his eye. "What happened between us, Con?" He looked at her intently as he said that and Connie knew he was serious.

"What makes you think I know, Matthew?"

"You know everything, dear sister, always did. I am not

the dunce you think I am. And I do care."

"I guess it started when I was 12. You had just come home from a tennis tournament and the trophy was on the dining room table. You and Dad dominated the conversation, tennis, tennis and more tennis. Mom just sat there and smiled. Her day had been more of what she always did, and when she opened her mouth it was about bridge, or meetings with her wealthy friends, snobbish talk about the DAR, snide remarks about the Jews, what she bought at Neiman's, never ever relating to what you and Dad were talking about. I just sat and listened, no one paying any attention to me. I didn't like sports, Mom and Dad didn't care about music or art. They gave me lessons; Mom had her driver, Jimmy, take me wherever I needed to go but rarely asked me about what was happening in my life."

"Play a little something for us, Constance."

"Not like a request that I could refuse, just do as I say whenever we had company. I never enjoyed it but I obeyed. So I turned away from the family, Matthew, withdrew into myself.

"I lived in a fantasy world of concerts and music, books, and drawing pictures of me playing in front of large audiences filled my mind. My piano teacher, Mrs. Neumann, a German refugee who survived the camps, became my confidant and friend. She took me to concerts by bus even though we had the use of Jimmy and the car. Once I noticed that she was wearing her dress inside out and when I told her she said, "It's entirely unimportant darling, it's only a dress. What matters is the heart beneath it."

"And you, Matthew, every month another win, another reward. I hated you for the attention you received and the silence about my accomplishments. I also hated you for how you cut the Tasty cakes we had sometimes. I was 16 before I realized that they had icing. You cut them in half all right but sideways, I got the bottom you got the top."

"I did that?" Matthew was grinning as he looked at his sister, trying to break the tension in her voice.

"You did. As we got older, when you went away to college and I spoke to Father about my education he let me know that in his mind women were homemakers, did not need to go further in their education. I wasn't surprised at his attitude; I guess I always knew that I was on my own in our house."

"When Dad entered politics we saw him less and less. Mom started to drink more and became a recluse. You were in the headlines for athletics and I had small notices in the paper, too, but Mom and Adam didn't notice, didn't care. I was a National Merit scholarship winner and left for Vassar when I was 18. I was lonesome but free.

"I met David at a dance sophomore year. We fell in love but I was terrified. He was Jewish and I knew how our parents felt about Jews. I began to refer to them as Adam and Susan, not Mom and Dad, just to myself when I thought about home.

"I spent vacations in New York with David and his family. For the first time in my life, I was included in conversations, intellectual conversations about the world and societal problems and solutions. Other than a Menorah on a shelf in the dining room, there were no signs of religion. No hanging crosses, pictures of Jesus or statues of Mary. When David or his parents asked me to play for them, I did so with pleasure and they appreciated what they heard. There was no doubt that we would get married and I volunteered to convert. They introduced me to Rabbi Davidson; I studied with him for a year and you know what happened after that. Adam and Susan never even acknowledged the wedding invitation and you came reluctantly, Matthew, but you came and I appreciated your being there. So that's the story."

Connie, relieved from the anxiety of facing her brother, leaned back on the chair, covered her eyes, and let out a long breath. It was a few minutes before she called room service to bring more coffee. They took the trays away and Matthew, staring out the window, began to talk.

"You know, Sis; I am a Christian to the core. Although I work for the Republican Party, I am paid by a foundation that is promoting a revolutionary change in America. We have the ear of every Christian denomination and access to the real powers in Washington. Big business runs our country, Con, big business and their lobbyists, not the elected officials. Moreover, big business is run basically by Christian fundamentalists today. What they want I am committed to finding ways and means to make happen. The letter you gave me, finding out Dad is half-Jewish half Catholic, doesn't faze me. So he is half the original and half the copy, so what? What is important is what I believe to be true. Jesus and his teachings must be followed if the world is to survive. It is written and, therefore, it is so."

"But what if it wasn't so, Matthew, what if the written history didn't happen that way?"

"What are you saying Connie, the Bible isn't the Bible?"

"It's a history written by men, and men don't always write what they saw or what is the truth, and that, dear brother, is a fact of life. Take the history of the war in Iraq today. The first so-called "fact" that sent us there was we were about to be attacked with weapons of mass destruction. The second was that Saddam is a threat to the world. The third, that without him we could have democracy in Iraq and bring stability to the region. The fourth, that the people of Iraq want democracy.

"Which of those histories that we have witnessed and are living through is the truth? And what will be written about it when we leave? What will the people read and rewrite in generations to come? That those we call insurgents today are the rulers of tomorrow, heroes who freed their nation from the Infidels?

"Wasn't that the history that was written in England in 1770? That is the history written in Israel in the 1940's about Menachem Begin and his Stern gang. They were called heretics 2000 years ago and killed for their beliefs. We are still killing for our beliefs, Matthew, especially the killings by the Muslims today and the Americans in Iraq.

"Don't you think that the teaching and preaching of the Church led to the Holocaust? Why? I cannot believe as you do that we all are born in sin and need salvation, that Abba, the father, sent his son to Earth to die and created a worshipful image. There is only one father, Matthew, the father of us all, within us all. Until mankind finds a way to resolve and accept that we will all remain enemies, willing to kill for our beliefs."

"Do you really believe all that, Connie? Isn't there any doubt in your mind?"

"Sure, I have some doubts. But my doubts are not as strong as your unbending beliefs. History as written is not necessarily the truth. Rabbi Davidson told me about a few experiences his dad had with historians. William Manchester wrote a book, his memoir, *'Out of Darkness'*, and described Iwo Jima being used as base for B-29's to bomb Japan; Doris Kearns Goodwin described the same scene in one of her books about the Roosevelts. ABC's Peter Jennings did a long segment on February 19, 1995, the fiftieth anniversary of the invasion and stated, "When Iwo Jima was taken the bombing of Japan began."

All of them were alive when Iwo was taken and the bombings of Japan took place and none of them got it right. The bombing of Japan began from China in November 1944 and escalated dramatically when bases were established on Guam, Tinian, and Saipan. Iwo was much too small to handle bombers, personnel, and equipment to sustain them. It was a fighter base and did not have a paved runway until May. Sam knew because he landed there on March 7, 1945 and did not leave until October. Manchester responded with a letter that said, "So what if I was wrong", Kearns never answered her letter and Jennings called him on the phone to thank him. So much for historians and some of what they write.

"I have so many questions, Matthew. If Jesus was Jewish, why do Christians hate Jews so much? If the first followers were all Jewish and those who wrote about him later were

Romans, why wouldn't the Romans blame the Jews for killing him? Can it be possible that the founders of the religion created the myths and the miracles? How can we talk about a Judaic/Christian tradition when Christians believe that only those who are baptized are welcome in heaven, there is no connection one to another whatsoever? I haven't found answers in Christianity, only what seems to be a faith in the myth of Jesus not the reality of what he stood for as a man."

"So what are we talking about, Connie? Religion? I am a Christian, you are a Jew? I change, you change? What?"

"Not even close, Brother dear. We are family whether you like it or not. If we cannot accommodate different thinking as two people without killing each other, how can we expect the world to survive? You in your devout unbending Christian beliefs that you want to impose on me, on America, and who knows where that will lead? What I want is to have a family again, not on my terms alone, but not on yours or Adam's either."

Chapter Seventeen

"Peter, it's Connie, Matthew and I would like to meet with you and then with Mark."

"Can the four of us meet at one time, Connie? It would make it easier for both of us."

"Sure, Peter, but where and when?"

"I'll talk to Mark and see if he is available tomorrow. There is a small Chinese restaurant, Ching Dao, around the corner from his parents' New York apartment, Third Avenue near 68th. If you do not hear from me, we will meet there for dinner at 7-tomorrow night. OK?" When Connie hung up Peter called Mark and arranged the meeting.

Connie and Matthew were standing in front of the restaurant when Peter and Mark arrived. Mark was taken by surprise by Matthew; he looked so much like his youngest brother, Lee. Matthew had a firm handshake and steady gaze, and Mark thought, "Here's a man of conviction, someone I might be able to like." But the conversation that ensued convinced Mark that Matthew would be difficult to even get to know, let alone change his attitude about how his faith might damage America.

Matthew began the conversation immediately after they all gathered and were still in front of the restaurant, "I am here only because Connie insisted that I meet the two of you. I read the letter, found it interesting, but see no reason to tell my father about it. No reason for me to get involved in spite of what my sister may want."

"He has always been stubborn and hard to bend," Connie added.

Matthew offered a quick handshake to Peter followed by a hug for his sister and the four of them followed the host to a small round table in the rear of the restaurant.

Mark was facing the picture window on 3rd Avenue and saw the Hebrew letters on a storefront, Beit Yisrael, across from where he sat. He knew it to be an Orthodox Synagogue whose Rabbi, Chiam Glazer, was politically active and raised money for Jews living in Gaza. Glazer was extremely vocal in his opposition to the Israeli Prime Minister's policies regarding the occupied land.

Mark had known Glazer in Israel when both were students. The fundamental, ultra religious right wing orthodox sect he belonged to was vocal in its opposition to the Israeli military. They believed that because the Bible was written in Hebrew it was the language of God, they refused speak it as a common language. They conversed in Yiddish or the language of the country they came from, mostly Russian or Polish. They refused to join the Israeli Army. When the war of 1967 became imminent, they barricaded the main road from Tel Aviv to Haifa with sand-filled 50-gallon oil drums as the sun went down on Friday nights. "Even the army must obey the Sabbath," they declared. Yet they defiled the Sabbath themselves when they instructed their children to throw stones at cars passing their Synagogue on the way to the beach on Saturdays.

In New York and other large cities, they used "Jew-mobiles," vans parked on busy street corners where they preached the word of God and tried to convert non-observant Jews to their way of life. Distinct in their black caftans and large black hats, they were an enigma to Mark.

When they were all seated, Mark asked Matthew how long he had been living in Washington.

"Just six months, since I got my Masters in marketing."

"Would you tell us what you do, Matthew?" Mark asked.

"Why? Is that important? Actually I feel that I am here to be interrogated and I resent that," he responded.

Connie, who had been looking directly at Mark, turned toward her brother and said in a quiet voice, "Matthew, we discussed this before we came to New York. Rabbi Davidson and Peter have convinced me that Adam should know about his background."

"It's just a Jew thing, Sis. Nothing very important!"

Both Peter and Mark looked at him, started to speak, when the bomb exploded in the Synagogue across 3rd Avenue.

Chapter Eighteen

The glass window in their restaurant blew out and small pieces shot through the room. Patrons screamed as they were hit by shards of flying glass. Fortunately, the booth in the back of the restaurant shielded them from injury. Peter had covered Connie when the explosion occurred; Matthew and Mark had remained motionless at the table. In minutes the wail of sirens filled the air then stopped as the fire trucks, ambulances and police cars arrived in front of the flaming store called Beit Yisrael.

Mark looked at Matthew in disgust as he recalled his last words. What they were witnessing at this very moment was "Just a Jew thing," too. Not very important? He pounded his fist on the table in frustration wondering what to say, what to do. It was Peter who responded to his thoughts as he looked at Matthew and said, "And what is this, Matthew?" as he handed him a sheet of paper that had blown into the restaurant.

CHRISTIANS FOR CHRISTIANITY IN AMERICA was

emblazoned on the top of the page. *Founded by Christians, America must return to Christianity as our founders wished. Abortion must be abolished, homosexuality extinguished and prayers in schools reestablished. We will not rest until our savior, Jesus Christ, is recognized as the redeemer of all that is good in the world.*

Matthew's face turned white as he looked at the paper. His hand trembled and his voice was just a whisper as he said, "I think I am going to be sick."

Peter helped Matthew into the rest room; Mark was holding Connie in his arms and comforting her when a police officer asked them to leave the restaurant.

Third Avenue was crowded with vehicles, hoses, and onlookers. Mark asked the police officer, "What happened, was anyone hurt?" The police officer told him that a young man on a bicycle had dropped off a package and sped away. He had planted a small bomb in the doorway of the synagogue. No one had been injured seriously but the fire and the water had caused some damage. "Just another nut case in New York," he said as he kept the onlookers moving along the sidewalk.

Peter and Matthew joined Connie and Mark a few minutes later and they walked in silence for several blocks. Mark was the first to speak.

"Just a little Jew thing! Nothing very important?" His

words were angry, sarcastic and meant to hurt, and they did.

Matthew buried his face in his hands, Connie reached out for her brother, and Peter said, "Not now, Mark. This is not the time or the place."

"If not now, Peter, when?"

"I'm leaving for Washington tomorrow to visit my mother," Peter replied. "Matthew and I are going to get together while I am there and we will have an opportunity to talk. I think it best that I am alone with him to see what actions he may or may not want to take. OK?"

Connie nodded her approval; Matthew grimaced and nodded his head in agreement. Mark did not pursue it any further. He trusted Peter and knew he would do all he could to help Matthew make a decision.

Connie and Matthew flagged a cab and left. Peter and Mark walked to their apartment, each deep in thought without any further conversation.

They said goodbye in the morning. Peter left for Penn Station and promised to call Mark after his meeting with Matthew.

As soon as Peter left, Mark picked up the phone and called Chiam Glazer at his home in Brooklyn. Chiam lived with his wife and three children on the third floor of his grandfather's home in the Williamsburg section of the borough. His father, Saul, was the rabbi at the adjoining

Synagogue and lived on the second floor of his father's house.

"Chiam, Its Mark Davidson. Are you all right?"

"Good of you to call, Mark. Did you read about the bomb?"

"Not exactly, I was eating Chinese across the street when it went off. Saw the whole thing. Thank God, no one was hurt. Do you know who did it, Chiam?

"The Peaceniks."

"Israelis, Chiam? Are you sure?"

"Of course."

"But why?"

"For the same reason Sadat was killed by his people and Rabin by mine, Mark. Ha Eritz, the Land. If we give an inch today, it only shows weakness. We must keep everything until the Messiah comes and he will tell us what God wants."

Mark was silent for some time before he spoke. "Chiam, I read the leaflet."

"Ah, yes, the leaflet. Who better to blame than the Goyim. Good night, Rabbi."

Mark looked at the phone in disgust, put it back on the cradle, shook his head in disbelief and murmured to himself, "Jews against Jews, Muslims against Muslims, Christians against Christians, and I am trying to find peace in a family?"

Chapter Nineteen

"This is where grown men come to cry." It was Peter talking to Matthew as they walked toward a bench in front of the Vietnam War Memorial; the long, black marble shrine glistened in the late afternoon sun.

"Not the Iwo Jima memorial, Peter?" Matthew asked.

"Iwo Jima was a battle, Matthew. It affected the nation, no doubt about that, but with pride. However, this black wall reflects a war that tore families apart, the country apart. I myself went from a being a silent spectator to becoming an activist in opposition to my government. I did not feel comfortable standing idle, preaching tolerance on Sundays while my family blindly followed the policies of Nixon. I agonized about my role in the church, sought out, and joined protest groups, yes, and even spent time in jail. My mother and father were distraught with my actions and told me so directly. It was years before we sat down for a family dinner again. When we did, I had resigned my priesthood, the war had ended, and all of these young men whose names are on this wall, were gone.

They sat on a bench, their backs to the setting sun. The faces of weeping men and women reflected off the stark marble shrine.

"I wanted to talk to you, Matthew; I wanted you to know about me, about Rabbi Davidson. When I am finished, you may have an insight into why our country is being split into pieces, being torn apart today, much as it was during Vietnam. I promise you, as we did Connie, that whatever the two of you decide to do about the letter will be the final decision. Mark has already told his father about the letter and you must decide if you want to tell yours. If it is not your wish to proceed, the letter will be destroyed."

Peter did not wait for a verbal answer; the slight nod by Matthew was enough for him to continue talking.

"Before I begin I want you to know something that I truly believe, Matthew, and that is this. All wars are fought for profit. Whether that profit be power, land, oil, gold, domination, or combinations of the above is not important. From my perspective and from others that I know, there is an internecine war being fought in the United States today for control of our country by religious fundamentalists. I do not want you to explain or defend, Matthew, just listen and take to heart what I say. OK?"

Again, Matthew nodded.

"Mark and I became tennis partners when we were 12 in New Jersey. We played together nearly every day for four years, indoors in the winter, outdoors the rest of the years. His father, Samuel, knew my father, who was a General at Fort Monmouth, and they played golf together. We played in state and national tournaments in singles and doubles and competed against your father every year for several years until I left for Germany right after I graduated high school. Mark continued to compete against Adam right through college.

"As a young man my father had dreams of becoming a priest. His loyalty to his religion was a source of strength and pride within him. But we were in the Great Depression and he needed to work to help support his family. He studied law at night school and took the only job he could find, with the government. That eventually took him to Washington and into the military as an Intelligence officer. He rose in rank and became a General. Like all professional soldiers, he lived by a code of behavior and loyalty. To get ahead in the military you obeyed orders and kept all negativity you might feel to yourself. You were to do or die, not to question why. This unbending loyalty was a way of life.

"That term, loyalty to the cause of the Church and to the military, was discussed in our house. In my heart, I know that my mother chose me to represent our family in the church. I was not an unwilling participant; I enjoyed being an altar boy and felt the pride and love of my mother when she saw me standing next to the priest on Sunday mornings. I thought my father approved too even though we had talked about my going to the Air Force Academy and becoming a pilot.

"As the years went by I vacillated between going to the Air Force Academy and going to the Seminary. I was torn between my mother's love for the church, her daily rituals and prayers, lighting candles, saying rosaries, bonding with her and the Catholic Church and trying to cement a bond with my father by joining the Air Force. I knew it would be easier for my mother if I accepted the Church, so that is what I did.

"I found that I liked being immersed in study, but I did not like only having contact with men. So I looked for another outlet and found it by writing, first poetry and then a novel.

"My vision expanded and my thought darkened when I read poems about B-52's dropping bombs across Vietnam and Cambodia. I questioned America's role in the war inwardly and fought the desire to explore my father's role in it. He was my father; he must know what he is doing, who am I to question? I even spent a night in jail as a Vietnam

War protestor.

"One of my professors opened my eyes to the fact that the Bible might be fiction. It took me quite awhile to accept that what I knew of Adam and Eve, Noah, David and Goliath, the parting of the Red Sea, heroic stories of the Bible might not be historical records. I had to accept the fact that the Roman Catholic Church was begun by scattered groups of Jews who sensed the presence of their Lord in their own acts of daily living. I read extensively, Matthew, especially books by religious writers in search of meaning. One writer, Hans Kung wrote *'Renewal and reform of the Church are permanently necessary because the Church consists first of human beings, and, secondly, of sinful human beings.'* That placed everyone connected to the Church in human terms that we were all the same regardless of the hierarchy.

"Cardinals, Popes Bishops, Priests, nor lay people were exempt from judgment. From that, I learned two things; first, no human being has the right to sit in absolute judgment of another. Second, the role of religion in our life and our relationship to God, and to each other, must be forgiveness. These principals became my guide and road map to who I am, what I do, how I think.

"My studies led me to recognize that the fear of living in Hell and not in Heaven is a powerful tool, Matthew. I began to feel that reward, punishment is un-Christian, like saying, good Christians receive, and bad Christians are punished. How can that be justified, good, and bad? Being a Christian means being a Christian, living like Jesus lived.

"The Church was like a government with a hierarchy that led to the Pope as a symbol of God. For the first time in my life, I had an understanding of the question, 'Why?' Why did others break away from Catholic faith? I had always thought the divisions among Christian denominations were scandalous. Then I began to understand the need to reform, to liberalize, to know the touch and love of a woman. I realized then that the sin we all feared, sex, was not necessarily the original sin our religion teaches. Our greatest sin is what the Bible calls the worship of false gods, the making of idols, golden calves. In today's world, we do not worship golden calves but we do worship our nation and our Church.

"That was not all, Matthew. Soon it became clear to me that even Jesus had been made into an idol. When I began to think of him as a fully human person, fallible and mortal, I questioned whether he ever considered himself divine. It startled me when I first realized that Jesus, our Lord, was never a Christian. Then, for the first time in my life, I saw Jesus as a man I could utterly identify with. I began to relate to him as somebody who lived a life worthy of emulation. I loved him more when I discovered his humanity, Matthew.

My religion became my guide to living on this earth.

"The events in the news in my younger days, The Bay of Pigs, the assassination of JFK, the Cuban missile crisis, the Vatican Council, the words of Hans Kung and the first stirrings of the sixties revolution, are no different from the events of today. Iraq, the religious division of America, global warming, Katrina, yes, and even terrorism both here and abroad, must be looked at by your generation much as mine looked at ours. We must trust in this life, this process, this history, wherever it takes you. Live without idols. The whole of life belongs to God. It *is* God.

"This was the religious education I received in the community of the seminary. The message of our faith, what I began to learn personally from my family, is trust, and I learned it as a student of theology as well. I was at peace with myself as a person and as a priest. Then I embarked on a course that would cause me to lose what I valued most of all, the trust, and bond with my father."

Chapter Twenty

"I brought my father here too, Matthew. He was quite old; a retired general whose job helped put 20,000 names on the face of this memorial. Somewhat senile, he stood by the wall rubbing his hands over the names looking for comrades he had known who were killed in Vietnam. When I asked him if I could help him he said 'No, just leave me be.' He had assumed the names were in alphabetical order as was the military procedure he had always known. I even had the feeling that he might have been trying to find his name as well.

"My father was a 'good man,' Matthew, What son doesn't think that of his father? But circumstances over which he had no control made me turn against him. I confronted him one time about the dropping of bombs on civilian targets. That had really bothered me then and does now.

"We are at war and we must do what we do to win. The pure purpose of fighting a war is to kill your enemy and that is what we are doing, was what he said and I had no answer for him.

"In time, more and more Americans began to protest the war and I did, too. First quietly and then, as the years went by, the protests became more frequent and much more visible. I walked in protest in front of the White House. I did it for me, for what I believed.

"One did not oppose a superior in the military. If asked, 'Can you?' the answer had to be 'Can do,' so my father had to follow through with the orders he received.

"In 1967 the Secretary of Defense, Robert McNamara, had concluded that the bombing was ineffective and that the war could not be won; but he never went public with this knowledge. My father finally could not carry on any longer, so he retired from the military. Shortly after his retirement, his physical and mental state changed dramatically, and, in fact, he never recovered all of his faculties.

Chapter Twenty-one

The sun had set behind them; the black granite shrine seemed to fade into the darkness when Peter and Matthew left the memorial. They walked to Peter's rented car in silence. It was fifteen minutes before Matthew said, "You triggered some powerful thoughts, Peter."

"That was my intention," Peter responded.

"Where are we going?"

"I know a small pub in Georgetown. We can get a good burger and a beer if that is OK with you?"

"Can we talk there?"

"Do you mean, is it quiet enough?"

Matthew smiled when he responded, "I don't speak such good English, do I?"

"We all express ourselves that way sometimes, but yes; we can get a booth and have some privacy."

They found a parking space near the Houndstooth, and took a booth in the rear of the nearly empty restaurant. It was after nine and they did not leave until eleven thirty.

Matthew, when pressed by Peter about his relationship with his father, had difficulty focusing on himself.

"I always was jealous of the relationship my sister had with my mom. Not only did she get all kinds of lessons, piano, painting, elocution, dancing and you name it. They just seemed to share so much. It was if I didn't exist when the two of them were together in the kitchen. They talked and laughed, went shopping at least once a week and Connie always seemed to get her way. Not that I was neglected, but father just wasn't home enough. We were living on the ranch, about 40 miles from Austin and he had an apartment in town near the Capitol. When he did come home on weekends the house filled up with politicians and business people seeking favors. The phone never stopped ringing; it was a mad house. I resorted to placing a note on the phone when I wanted to or needed to talk to him

"He did have his own plan for raising his son, reward for accomplishments, especially in athletics, and punishment for failures. I received money for good grades, for hits in baseball, touchdowns in football and baskets in basketball. He knew what I was doing through the papers and from Mom. I don't think he ever saw me play until we played football for the State championship on a Friday night in Austin. I knew he was there and I really wanted to make the big play, get his attention. I was thinking so hard about him that I could not concentrate on the game at all. The coach benched me in the 4th quarter; my replacement scored the winning touchdown. I was mortified and father never noticed. He was just happy that we won.

"I started drinking after that last game. It got out of control when I was a junior at Texas U. Another guy on the football team was with me when I drove into a concrete pole on the freeway. His injuries were permanent and I did not have a scratch. The headlines screamed about Adam Flowers' son, that embarrassed him more than the concerns I thought he should have had for me, and he let me know that loud and clear. I knew then for sure that I did not have a father I could count on. Fortunately, Coach Hayes introduced me to the Fellowship of Christian Athletes and I let Jesus take control of my life. Some months after the accident, in his way of apology, my father told me, 'I am just like my grandfather and my father, Matthew. We enjoy planting seeds but hate to take care of the crops.'

"He actually thought he was being funny but I knew he was serious," Matthew said. "Then he began to talk to me about his father and grandfather"

"My grandfather, Preston," he began, "was a hardnosed son-of –a-bitch, who started working in the oil fields when he was 12 and had a knack for preaching that was overwhelming. He could talk people out of or into anything, and he did. When he was 16, he started collecting oil leases from farmers. Once when he was after one large piece of land in west Texas and couldn't talk the farmer into giving him a lease, he pursued and married the farmer's daughter. That land is still producing and will continue to for generations to come."

Matthew continued speaking but now he had a distant look in his eyes, as if he was sitting in a room listening to his father speak. "His grandfather never worked on Sunday and attributed his success to his belief in Christ and the Bible. My grandfather, Barry, once told my father that the bible was his father's guide and that he had always had one in his hand when he was talking to land owners about giving him leases. He hardly ever laughed but he did have a twinkle in his eyes when he told Adam that story.

"When Barry was born, Preston was an extremely wealthy man with no background with children. Preston's parents had died when he was 5 or 6 and he was raised by foster parents until he ran away when he was 14. His life was his business. My great grandmother, Alice, was the farmer's daughter he married to get land. She loved the earth and had a green thumb. She kept Barry at her side when she planted and harvested. Barry wasn't a momma's boy but he needed a father as we all do and he didn't have one. When he was 18, he forged his parents' names and joined the Marines two days after Pearl Harbor.

"My grandfather loved the military life. He found his calling, his home and blossomed into a man's man. His leadership skills were evident to his superiors and he rose rapidly through the ranks and into officers' training. He met my grandmother, Kate, at a dance and married her just before he shipped out to Hawaii and combat in 1942. He fought on Tarawa and Makin where he won the Silver Star for his actions. He came back to San Diego in late 1943 as a Captain, and then left again for the Pacific in 1944. His division was the first to land on Iwo Jima on February 19, 1945. A Japanese hand grenade wounded him just 3 days into the fight for that island. He had a long and difficult recovery. His left leg was amputated and his internal wounds took a long time to heal. That is when I was conceived."

Later, Peter told Connie and Mark that Matthew's face expressed awe and amazement when he shouted, "Holy shit, Adam doesn't even know that Barry is not his father. The letter!"

"And you do, Matthew, you read the letter," Peter spoke softly. What are you going to do about it?"

"I don't know."

"Do you like your father, Matthew?"

"No, I don't like him as a father, but I admire him for

what he believes."

"Which is?"

"He believes that Jesus is our savior. He believes that the Bible is the actual word of God, that we can lead the World to peace and harmony if everyone accepts that as his truth. And I believe it, too."

"Adam has stated publicly on many occasions that his hero is Jesus Christ. Do you think so as well, Matthew?"

"Of course, how else can I do what I am doing if I don't believe that?"

Peter leaned back into the booth, took a sip of the Guinness, and began to talk in a very soft voice.

"When I was a sophomore in college one of my professors began his first lecture by stating that he could not teach us anything. All that he could do was expose us to knowledge, knowledge that he had gained from a lifelong pursuit of reading, listening, experimenting as well as what others knew, taught, wrote about, and lectured on. That a good teacher was willing to expose himself by telling all he knew, all he felt and that his exposure would be genuine, from the heart and the head. And that a good student would take all of that in and then take what resonated within him and use that knowledge for his betterment. In that way, my professor said, 'I will achieve immortality for I will have given someone something that I exposed him to that he or she has used and possibly, passed on to others.'

"So, Matthew, I have told you about my family. Now I would like to tell you about me, about what I have learned in my 60 years of living on this planet. I am telling these things to you in the spirit of my professor. I, too, believe in Jesus with all of my heart. But there is more than one Jesus, Matthew. There is the Jesus that God created and there is the Jesus that man created.

"The Jesus that walked the Earth was Jewish, by birth, by knowledge and by actions. He had a passion for the truth as he saw it. Perhaps it was somewhat different then. Torah as he had learned it was what he believed. But he also believed in what he had been taught by the Rabbis. That one overriding fact is the goodness of man. If, as man believes today, that Jesus was a product of a Virgin birth, then one must believe that Joseph and Mary never consummated their marriage and that God was Jewish. How can one believe otherwise? There is no factual evidence that Joshua-ben-Joseph, Joshua son of Joseph, as he was known in Israel of that time was the son of God. He was born as you and I were born. He walked this Earth as an enlightened man and had a following. His heroism was his knowledge that he was a danger to the Romans and that he faced death by crucifixion. One thing we know for sure, Jesus was never a Christian. He never stopped preaching as a Jew. His death and reputed resurrection prompted a religion, created by men. That religion, your religion and mine, was threatened by the very existence of Jews. The writings of the Old Testament were discarded as being 'out of date,' and the New Testament was written over the next centuries.

"In the year 356 the Emperor of Rome, Constantine, had a vision or a dream of a cross. He took that as sign to accept Christianity as the religion of Rome and the Cross as the symbol of Christianity. He, too, was afraid of what was happening in Jerusalem and sent his armies, under the sign of the cross, to kill the Jews in Jerusalem. That pattern of wiping out the Jews as the killers of Christ persisted throughout the ages.

"The crusaders had crosses on their tunics as they plunged their blades into Jews and Muslims in 1056 and again 50 years later. Those crosses were symbols of the sword, not symbols of the cross Jesus died on, Matthew. A thousand years later the Church watched as Hitler, born a Catholic, killed six million Jews. That there are any Jews alive at all is one of God's miracles. Anti-Semitism persists today even though there are only 12 million Jews in the World of 6.3 billion people, .02 percent. Only a third of the population of the world is Christian. That we fear and threaten the Jews' existence is a testament to the inadequacies of our Church and its teachings. We look at the

Ten Commandments and mock them. We kill, we worship idols, and then Jesus absolves us of our sins. It seems that we can do anything and not be responsible for our sins. We have taken control of Heaven for those that are baptized and condemn those who aren't to an afterlife in an eternal Hell. I guess, as the rabbis write, that the big difference between us can be found in what we all know as the Golden Rule. "Do unto others as you would have them do unto you," as preached in Christianity, gives us the right by dint of power, of riches and might, to do anything we please and then be absolved of our wrong doings by confession. Our Golden Rule creates action and the Jews say, "Do not do anything to others that you would not have them do to you." And that presents them with a choice of inaction, more of making a choice to what is right before they take any action."

"So this is a Jewish thing, Peter, our talking is all about that?"

"Is that what you are thinking?"

"Yes, Peter, it is and it makes me quite angry."

"If that were all that the letter meant, Matthew, I wouldn't be here with you. My concerns are about the survival of humanity. America is on a path that may create a permanent state of war; a religious war based on whose God is God. "

"There is only one God, Peter. You and I know that."

"That's a Christian's view, Matthew, not necessarily the views of the other four billion people Christians share the planet with. And our actions, American actions as Christians, may affect the entire world if we view the world only through the eyes of the Christian Church. If you and Adam, and Samuel cannot reconcile and become a family, even a family with different views, then what chance do we have of the survival of all of humanity as a family? The Christians who came here for religious freedom first killed the red men, then enslaved the black men and imported the yellow men to do their dirty work and then wrote laws to keep them from becoming citizens. All of that was done in the name of God. Jesus, were he here would be appalled, Matthew. That bracelet with WWJD (what would Jesus do) on it is not the answer, what will Matthew do, is."

"Peter, I am only half your age and only a practicing Christian for 10 years, but I know this, I will not abandon my faith in my Lord Jesus and that is what you are asking me to do. My mother and father have shaped my world just as their world and yours was shaped by your parents. I see no reason to tell my father that Barry and Kate were not his birth parents. Nor do I see myself abandoning the people I work with or the principals we stand for. You and Connie may be disappointed, Peter, but a Christian nation with Christian values that follows the Bible is what I want to see happen, will work my ass off for, just as my father is doing."

"You miss the point entirely, Matthew. Christianity requires conditions, conditions of beliefs and faith that may not be based on fact. Values are universal and we must all have similar values. The faith that you have is the very reason that we should not have a national religion. Deep faith destroys humanity because it makes one feel superior. Many of those who loved Jesus passionately used that passion as a reason to kill and that, my friend, has been the history since his death.

"It must stop now or we will have no world. I am reminded of a quote from a German Lutheran pastor, Martin Niemoeller, when he was asked why he didn't speak out, take a stance when the Jews were being carted away, *"First they came for the communists, but I was not a communist, so I did not speak out. Then they came for the socialists and the trade unionists, but I was neither, so I did not speak out. Then they came for the Jews, but I was not a Jew, so I did not speak out. And then they came for me, and there was no one left to speak out for me."*

Matthew had ordered ginger ale with his rare hamburger, Peter a Guinness draft. They ate in near silence as Matthew remembered the taste of beer with a burger that he had loved so much. After the waiter had cleared the table, Peter began to speak and Matthew began to tap his thigh with his fingers. First, slowly then faster and finally his fingers curled into a fist in anger. How, he thought, could this man be so opposed to the Christianity I know and love? Matthew's anger abated somewhat when he remembered what Coach Hayes told him on the way to his first meeting of the Fellowship of Christian Athletes. "I know you are angry and I want you to know that anger is the first sign of denial. But it also is the first step to recovery, of acceptance."

Matthew looked Peter square in the eye and began to speak in a low, deliberate tone, "I have my passion, Peter, and I will not give it up. I am a Christian and an American and I believe they go together; one religion, one nation, one nation under God. When they start teaching Intelligent Design in schools, which they will be doing soon, we will be fulfilling the thoughts and dreams of Jesus. I want to be a part of my Lord's resurrection."

Part Two

Chapter Twenty-Two

Mark's phone began ringing at 6:30 while he was doing his morning meditation. He answered it at 7.

"Rabbi Davidson?"

"Yes."

"This is Jack Fox, Washington correspondent for the *Times*. The press were handed the presidents' schedule an hour ago. Samuel Davidson's name is on it for a 9 AM news briefing. He is your father, is he not? Do you know why he will be giving a briefing?"

"Yes, Jack, he is my father and all that I know is that he went to Washington yesterday. He didn't tell me why and I wouldn't tell you even if I did know."

"Are you surprised that he is meeting with the president?"

"Frankly, I am. He has been very vocal about his opposition to the president's choice for chief justice that puts five Catholic justices on the Supreme Court and the teaching of Intelligent Design in our public schools. I thought he was going to Washington to voice his feelings to the Senate. I guess I was wrong."

"How old is the judge now, Rabbi?"

"He will be 84 in February."

"Active? Healthy?"

"You bet. He walks every day, lifts weights, and plays a little golf. He is healthy, Jack. Complains about some about aches and pains and once in awhile that he can't do some of the things he used to enjoy. But his mind is as sharp as ever and he hasn't lost his sense of humor as corny as that is. He's OK."

"Thanks, Rabbi Davidson. Do you mind if I call you after the briefing this morning?"

"Not at all."

There were times when Mark regretted being a bachelor times when he would like to have someone to talk to over breakfast. This was one of those times. Strange, he thought, how the decisions of a twenty- one year old young man could have such an effect on a 60 year old man.

Mark always enjoyed the company of women when he was in college and formed a relationship with Audrey Rosin, a Penn cheerleader in his sophomore year. By the time they were juniors they had fallen in love and looked forward to marriage, children, and a long life together after graduation. Mark was an attentive, considerate young man and Audrey responded by offering herself to him a few months after they began dating. They enjoyed themselves immensely in everything they did together.

Audrey, unbeknown to Mark, took tennis lessons and surprised him when she carried her racket to the courts one day. Mark, generally a patient man with her, had to curb his lack of enthusiasm for playing with anyone with so little natural talent, but he did. Gradually, he looked forward to 'Tennis with Audrey,' and invented games that helped keep his interest. At times he played as a lefty, he would play the doubles lines on his side of the court and she the singles scoring a game for every point she made. It became a weekly event and they laughed through the hours on the court, the trips to the beach afterwards and the quiet, tender nights on most weekends that Mark was not at a tournament. Mark bought a ring and planned to give it to Audrey at graduation.

In his senior year, Mark knew he would be leaving for Jerusalem later in the summer to attend his first year of rabbinical school. He did not think it wise for Audrey to go with him or for them to get married until he was ordained and found a job. When he was sharing his memories with Peter he recalled, "I wasn't going to start my profession and the unknowns of married life at the same time, Peter. Didn't think either would be easy and together, well, that would be impossible.

"We were walking on the beach in Deal when I pulled the ring out of my pocket, stopped at the water's edge, and handed it to Audrey. Not very romantic, I know, but I had been carrying it for so long and that seemed as good a place and time so I stopped, handed her the box, knelt on the sand, and asked her to marry me.

"Audrey opened the box, put the ring on, pulled me up, and gave me a big hug as she whispered yes. About a dozen people were watching that scene unfold and began clapping and shouting 'Yes' I hadn't been aware that anyone was watching and felt slightly embarrassed but very happy. My happiness was short lived though. As we walked, I told Audrey that it would be at least three years before we could plan a wedding."

"Why?" she asked.

"I told her as gently as I could but she objected saying, I don't want to wait that long, Mark. We should get married now and I can help support us until you are ordained. We discussed it for two months with neither finding it in our hearts to compromise or change. The engagement was broken and I left for Jerusalem to begin my studies."

"As the years go by, I often think about what I might have missed and then counter with all that I have gained. My spiritual path certainly did not follow the norm. The few years that I had a congregation were difficult for me. I just didn't fit into that routine gracefully. I was more comfortable studying, seeking God instead of ministering to his flock. Being true to myself might have been selfish but it was my choice and I have contributed to humanity in ways that have proven meaningful. Seeing some of the troubled kids I coached turn their lives around turned mine around too.

"Each experience has brought me closer to the God of the Universe and separated me from the God of religion. When I close my eyes in prayer or meditation I experience the deep silence of connectivity to my surroundings and to Nature that formed us, sustains us, and keeps us whole.

"Life is so strange. When I broke off with Audrey, I stopped thinking about women, about sex. Actually I have been celibate ever since. When you, my friend Peter, left the priesthood you found a soul mate, married and now have three children."

Chapter Twenty-Three

At nine Mark called Peter to tell him a news report was about to be broadcast on C-Span, he wasn't home; this was another one of those moments Mark didn't relish being alone.

At 9:05 the President and Samuel appeared on the screen walking to the lectern in front of the Rose Garden. Lillian and Paul, the Davidson' grandson, were slightly behind them. The president began by thanking the press for coming then, turning toward Samuel, he said, "I am honored to be in the presence of such a fine American. He served our country as a fighter pilot in World War two, who married his childhood sweetheart, Lillian, 60 years ago, raised a fine family, and served as a Federal judge on the bench for nearly 40 years. My father used to say that when you want to get a job done give it to a fighter pilot. They are mission oriented and they focus on their mission until it is accomplished.

"I have not had such good press lately, and yes, I might have made a few mistakes, Katrina for one. But I need some answers to some questions that the press and the public have been vocal about even though I firmly believe that I am right...as I usually am. Those questions arose when I advocated teaching Intelligent Design as an adjunct to Darwinism in our public schools.

"Some of the older guys in my cabinet thought I should get some opinions on that subject before I asked Congress to pass a law that would fund bringing Christian scholars into our classrooms. I generally listen to what they say and that is the reason we are here this morning. I have decided to open hearings on Intelligent Design and have appointed Judge Samuel Davidson as special investigator. Judge Davidson has demonstrated repeatedly over the years that his personal views do not interfere with his decisions based on law and precedent. He will have the power to subpoena whomever he chooses and to pursue a line of questioning of his own choice.

"This will not be an inquisition, there will be no legal solutions for witnesses who choose not to co-operate or answer questions. I am hoping that those who do appear before Judge Davidson will provide sufficient evidence to allow him to make the decision to go forward with my plan. Judge, do you have anything you want to say?"

"Thank you, Mr. President, I think you have stated the goals of this journey quite succinctly and I have no need to add any more at this time. I would, however, like to tell everyone why I accepted this assignment and it had nothing to do with my being a fighter pilot. I am quite comfortable with my life as it has been unfolding and I am quite reluctant to change all of that. But it is very difficult to say no to a request by a President.

"For those of you who do not know him, the young man standing next to my wife is my grandson, Paul Davidson. He is one of the young, smart, inquisitive young people who inhabit the Earth today and he and Lillian speak about spiritual things often. He said to me, Grandpa, you should do this for all of us who question our existence. Why we are here, why we fight wars, why we go against the intelligence of Nature, the Laws of Nature." I am here to see if there are answers to his questions and those that he has raised in me by asking me his. I hope I can satisfy him, the president, and myself. Thank you very much."

When Samuel was finished speaking, the reporters began shouting questions at the president and Judge Davidson as they walked away waving their hands. They both stopped short when someone fired a question, "Why a Jew, Mr. President?"

"Who asked that?" The president replied in an angry voice.

"I did, sir, Jack Fox from the *Times*."

"It figures. Well, Mr. Fox, who better than a man who will scrutinize the issue from every side and get me off the hook for being one- sided on religious issues," and he began walking away.

Samuel had his arm around Lillian and Paul was talking to the President when the screen stopped showing the picture.

Mark finally reached his father by phone at his home in Florida two days after the C-Span broadcast from Washington. "How did this happen, Dad?"

"The White House operator called last Wednesday and told me the President wanted to speak to me. I was skeptical until I heard him say, 'Judge Davidson, this is the President, how are you?'

"Fine, sir," I answered.

'Let me tell you why I called, Samuel. I need some one of your stature to chair a commission on Intelligent Design. I am asking you to be that person.'

"With all due respect, Mr. President, I am not one of your big fans. I do not agree with you about Iraq, about most of your policies, about where this country is heading. I cannot see any reason that you should want me to chair a committee of any kind, let alone one on a subject I oppose."

'Look, Samuel, I know all those things. Just come up here to Washington and spend an hour with me before you say no. I will have a plane pick you up at 9 tomorrow morning and get you back to Florida in time for dinner. OK?'

"I thought about it for a minute or two, which is a long time when you are talking to the President, Mark. Then I said 'I have one caveat, sir, that I can bring a court reporter.'

Don't trust me Judge?

No sir, let me rephrase that, Mr. President, I don't trust myself. I am just used to having transcripts of important meetings and cannot get out of the habit. If it is a problem, I won't come.

"I don't see that as a problem, Samuel, just a bit unusual. See you tomorrow."

"I flew up in a small military passenger jet. I actually sat in the co-pilot's seat and handled the controls for a few minutes. It sure felt good seeing the horizon from a cockpit again, Mark."

There was a car waiting at Andrews and I arrived at the White House at 11:45 for our 12 o'clock meeting. I have to tell you that it is very difficult to turn down any request when you are in the Oval Office. I had given the subject a lot of thought and after we shook hands, I introduced Etta Waltzer, my stenographer, and said, "Mr. President, I told you I would come so I did. But I have to tell you that I am not your man. I think you want me because I am Jewish and a Democrat and that my appointment would serve you for political reasons."

He started to laugh as I was talking and said, 'Why else do people in Washington do things, Samuel? There are always underlying reasons. You have served as a Federal judge and your personal opinions or your own beliefs have never interfered with your abilities or swayed your opinions. I am a God- fearing man, Samuel but I believe in the righteousness of man.'

"That, too, separates us, Mr. President. I do not fear God, only love him. I once heard a case where a Mafia leader was asked, 'Do your underlings love you or fear you?' 'They fear me,' he said, 'and that is the way I want them to behave. Their fear motivates them to be wary of me, kept on edge, never knowing how I will respond to any of their actions. If they love me I can't punish them, keep them in line.' I have never forgotten that, sir, and I see that as a very major difference between you and me, Christians and Jews."

"Well, Samuel, you do take a firm stance. What do you know about Intelligent Design?"

"Not much, Mr. President. But ....I better not say any more."

"No, go ahead."

"Well, sir, in most instances anything that you are for, I am against."

"That's the way I feel about Democrats, Sam. But it is our

country and we should be able to have this dialogue in a confidential manner. Now let's get back to the issue, your President is asking for your help. What do you say?"

"Frankly, sir, I do not think this is the right time to air anything about Intelligent Design. There is a trial about to start in Pennsylvania and any undue publicity may interfere with that case."

"Well put, Samuel, however we believe that all the publicity we can generate will be helpful to the nation's understanding."

"Under those conditions, Mr. President, I cannot refuse. But I must tell you, my investigation and report may not be what you want to hear, but it will be an analysis of what I uncover."

"Good," was all he said.

"At that point he stuck out his hand, we shook, and, while still holding my hand, he ushered me out of the office. I landed back in Tampa at 4 that afternoon."

Chapter Twenty-Four

The Jewish holidays were early in June and Mark wanted to see his Mom and Dad, especially his father. He wanted to talk to his father about a possible conflict of interest if Adam Flowers was called upon to testify and he knew that his parents were always were lonesome for family on Rosh Hashanah and Yom Kippur. When he told them he was coming, they were delighted. Mark asked them to pick him up at the airport in St. Petersburg, only 30 minutes from their home on the beach. Delta had started a new service from New York and that spared his parents from driving to Tampa from their home.

It was October and the weather had started to change in Florida; the days were cooler, not so humid, so father and son played a few rounds of golf at Sandridge, walked the beach, and talked. Mark expressed his feelings that having Adam testify might be a conflict of interest. Samuel alleviated his son's concerns when he said, "If he knew that I was his father I would not have agreed to take this on, Mark.

That he doesn't know will not interfere with my line of questioning and certainly can have no influence on his answers."

"It's a no-win setup for you, Dad," Mark exclaimed. "If you write an opinion for ID in schools, the president will make capital out of your being Jewish and a liberal Democrat. If you write in opposition he will use the same reasoning in denouncing your opinion."

"I know that, Mark, so I have a transcript of our first meeting to use in case it comes to that. The first hearing is scheduled on October 17 in the small Senate hearing room at the Capitol."

Curious as to who was going to testify and how they were going to be approached, Mark asked, "Who are you going to subpoena?"

Samuel laughed and said, "Subpoena? The White House has a list of 500 callers already and I had to shut off my phone. I will have a long list. Two that have agreed already are Adam Flowers and Rabbi Ross. Adam called the President and I asked the Rabbi. I thought about his sermon in 1960, I thought he would be as eloquent on this subject as he was on that. Like then I don't know his position but I have such respect for the man, for his intellect and judgment that I just had to have him on the stand."

"If Rabbi Ross wrote that sermon today it would be 'Can

any voter vote for a Fundamental Christian to be President?' I think his answer would be a resounding No! But that aside, Dad, don't you think you are being used?"

"Of course, that's why I accepted. I think the hearing will end after the first or second day because the president won't like what he hears. His excuse will be the trial in Dover, Pennsylvania, where the School Board is being sued to stop the teaching of Darwinism exclusively."

Chapter Twenty-Five

Mark, his mother and Peter were in the gallery when Judge Davidson entered the Senate hearing room. Reporters and photographers crammed together on the floor in front of the dais. The bright lights from C-Span focused on the front of the room and the table where the first speakers, Adam Flowers and Rabbi Ross, were seated behind the speakers' table. Samuel took his seat, adjusted the microphone, turned to Etta, and asked if she was ready. When she nodded yes, he began. "Good morning to you all. I am Samuel Davidson. I am here today at the request of the President of the United States. As you know the president and others are talking about teaching Intelligent Design in schools along with the theories of evolution as proposed by Charles Darwin. Some in Congress even believe that ID should be taught exclusively.

"Although I have specific beliefs about the subject, I can assure you that my 40 years as a judge in courts across this country have taught me the discipline necessary to eliminate personal opinions on a host of subjects including religion and science. All judges are human, all humans have opinions, and we are no exception.

"I am not here to judge but to inquire, to write an opinion and give that opinion to the President for him to use as he sees fit. Believe me when I tell you, there is no shortage of people from every occupation who want to speak here. I have set a limit of two speakers a day, each with 3 hours.

"You will hear from a few elected officials, some religious leaders, some scientists, and some lay people. There will only be ten speakers as we have to end these sessions in one week. I will introduce the speakers, ask them to give a little of their background and then I will ask each speaker the same first question, do you believe in Intelligent Design and what is your definition of ID? This is not an inquisition. There will be no swearing in as all of the speakers are here on their own cognizance and all are eager to be heard. So let's begin by asking Senator Adam Flowers to take his place in front of the microphone."

Adam stood up, straightened his tie, buttoned his jacket, and took a seat at the table. Mark looked at him intently and thought he was bigger, taller than he had remembered, his face was unlined, and his hair graying and unruly. He was handsome in a masculine way and very well dressed.

"Good morning, Senator, I haven't been in your presence

for more years than I care to remember, I do hope you are well."

"Quite well, Judge Davidson, and it is nice to see you again. How is Mark?"

"You can ask him yourself a little later," and pointed to where his son was sitting.

"Are you ready to begin?"

Adam nodded and Samual asked, "Do you believe in Intelligent Design and what is your definition of ID."

"I am a Christian, sir, and I believe that we were created by God. Intelligent Design is, simply put, that everything we are, everything we think, are gifts from God, we owe our lives to him in the literal sense and his son died so we could live a better life."

"In your beliefs, Senator, is there a time frame for that creation?"

"According to the Bible it was when Adam and Eve were created. I don't know the year, nor do I think that a year has ever been specified if that is what you mean."

"So, actually you believe that all of humanity as we know it today evolved from two people."

"Yes."

"How?"

"What do you mean, how?

"What I mean, Senator, is where did the next generation

come from? Did Adam and Eve copulate? And then, after twenty or thirty years did their children copulate? And so on until there were 3 or 4 million people on Earth at the time 2000 years ago when Jesus was born? And if what you are saying is true, what did the designer look like and what did those two people look like?"

"I never gave that any thought nor do I believe I was ever exposed to that question before. But I would have to assume what you just said is what actually happened. The Bible says that God created us in his image, so they must have looked like you and me."

"White like you and me, sir, or-----?"

"White like you and me, Judge," he answered with his lips closed tight, blood rushing to Adam's face as this line of questioning began.

"So, you believe that God is white, Senator? Is that what I am to understand?"

"Yes, that is what I believe."

"Is that your personal belief or is that what you have been taught through reading the Bible."

"The Bible has been and is my guide, sir."

"Would I be correct then if I said that you believe that all of humanity has the same father, one creator?"

"Isn't that what you believe? What Jews believe?"

"What I believe isn't the issue. What I am trying to find

out is what the proponents of Intelligent Design want to teach our children in school. I have always learned more from my children than I could ever teach them. I ask that question of you as a father asking a son."

"But you are not my father, Judge Davidson."

Judged Davidson hesitated before he said "You are my teacher today, Senator Flowers, and I am learning from you. Do you wish to continue, sir? You are here by choice and you can end this interview at any time."

Adam gestured to continue the questioning.

"So the answer to my question then is that we all have one father, the creator and that in Biblical times, everyone on Earth was white."

"I can't vouch for the color question, actually there is no way of knowing is there? But, yes we all have one father, one creator."

"Of course, we can vouch for the color question and we do know about race in biblical times, Senator. Science has the answers and those answers do not agree with ID. However, if Intelligent Design is taught in schools will you want to use the Bible as a guidebook in the literal sense? I must remind you, I am only gathering information, not judging the validity of what I am learning. To continue, Senator, doesn't the Bible tell the story of Moses, too; the burning bush, the Ten Commandments, the parting of the

Red Sea? Doesn't it tell of the covenant God made with Abraham and the people of Israel?"

"Yes, it does."

"Then couldn't you call the Ten Commandments the designer's manual for how to live one's life and that up until the time of Jesus had been used by Jews to guide and conduct their lives?"

"That sounds reasonable, sir."

"We should take a fifteen minute break. However, before we do I would like to summarize what Intelligent Design advocates want to teach in our schools. If I heard correctly, we are all descendants of two people and their descendents who were created by God in his image. That God and those who followed in Biblical times were white and all the stories in the Bible happened exactly as they are told. Is that a correct summary, Senator Flowers?"

"I am not unaware of your inferences, your honor, but, yes that is basically what I have said."

"One more question before we take a break, sir. Do you have any evidence to back up your beliefs?"

"I don't need any evidence, judge, it is a fact!"

"Thank you, we will reconvene in fifteen minutes."

The hallway was crowded, reporters were trying to speak to Adam when Mark walked over to him and stuck out his hand. He hesitated a moment, took his hand and said, "Mark?"

"Yes, Adam, it has been a long time hasn't it?"

"I wouldn't have recognized you, Rabbi. I called you "Rabbi" a long time ago didn't I? Guess I was prophetic."

"Then it was sarcasm, Adam, now it is the truth."

"Your father is a tough old bird, Mark, a smart, tough old bird."

"First he's a lawyer, Adam, and lawyers never ask questions to which they don't already know the answer. As I see it he's only asking you to tell the truth as you see it, as it is written."

"I know that, but what he isn't asking is what bothers me. It's like I am making his case for him and I don't like that at all."

"Since when is this his case? It is more yours than his is. You are the salesperson trying to sell educators a package, not he. If he were the buyer, you would have been out the door already. Good luck the rest of the morning." Mark returned to the meeting room just as his father walked in and sat down behind the microphone.

"What does the Bible say about the birth of Christ, Senator?"

"It says that a male child was born to the Virgin Mary, through an Immaculate Conception."

"Mary was married to Joseph at the time?"

"So it is written."

"So God picked out a married woman who had never consummated her marriage and after the birth of Jesus she was venerated as the Virgin Mary?"

"Everyone knows that story, Judge, even you."

"True, Senator, but what was their religion?"

"They were Jews, sir."

"Then God was Jewish, Senator?'

"Is that speculation on your part, Judge?"

"No, Senator, logic. The Jews were the first to practice a monotheistic religion. In Biblical times the Romans, the Egyptians and others worshipped many Gods. You know that but since I have only read, not studied, your Bible I do not know what references are made to other people, other religions, or to people of color in other parts of the world. So I have to ask you and will ask others these questions purely in the context of using the Christian Bible as a textbook in schools and for the promotion of the Christian religion as a national religion in America. But I am ahead of myself, Senator. Can you tell me when, in relationship to the birth of Jesus, Adam and Eve appeared?"

"I cannot. I would like to know why time is so important, sir."

"My goal in this hearing is to separate fact from fiction, myth from reality so that what we teach our children can be substantiated. In order to do that I need some semblance of a date of "the beginning" so I can work forward and see how long it would take two people producing heirs could produce enough humans to reach today's population of 6.3 billion people. I am sure that you will want your grandchildren to know the truth, Senator."

"Of course, Judge Davidson, but my son is a bachelor and I may never have that pleasure."

"Don't you have a daughter, Senator?"

"My personal life is not open to discussion here, sir. As to your question, I cannot see how it is relevant to Intelligent Design."

"I am trying to determine, Senator Flowers, if the Bible, the Christian Bible, includes the entire population of the Earth, from the first human on, or just white followers of Christianity. In other words, did God create humanity or just a portion of humanity?"

"I believe the Bible tells us that all were created by God but only those who accept Jesus as their savior can enter the Kingdom of Heaven."

"I find that interesting, Senator. Those who follow the dictates of the Father, the Designer, are excluded from spending there afterlife with him but those who follow the Son are not. Is that what you want our young people to learn? Never mind, Senator that is a rhetorical question and the answer is obvious. Can you tell me how Christianity got started, sir?"

"Jesus preached a gospel that was different from the Judaism he had learned as a young man. His preaching attracted a following and infuriated the established priests and holy men. They conspired with the Roman rulers to have him killed, crucified. This was God's plan, to have his son die for all of the sins committed by man."

"So you want our children to learn that God, the designer, who gave the commandment "Thou Shall Not Kill," to his chosen people, fathered a son knowing that the son was going to be killed, to be used as a sacrifice to establish Christianity?"

"That is what the Bible says, Judge. As it is written, so it must be, so it should be taught."

"Let's get back to the Bible, Senator. We cannot agree on the time of the beginning of humanity, perhaps we can agree on the date of the last entry in the Bible. Can you tell me when in the history of the World that was?"

"No Judge, I can't. I am sure that the writing continued after the death and resurrection, but I am not able to tell you when it ended."

"Should the teaching of ID include the history of Christianity up to and including the present day and should America have a national religion?"

"My answer to the first half of your question, sir, is I don't know but if we ever do have a national Religion then the history of Christianity will be taught. As it stands today, our country is about 80% Christian. We have a national religion by a wide margin without having it legislated. Our actions are Christian actions by Christian leaders who meet regularly in prayer and goodwill. We study the Bible, are loyal to our country and grateful to Jesus for his love and his guidance. Does that answer your question, sir?"

"Quite succinctly, Senator Flowers, thank you for your time. We will adjourn until 2 PM."

Chapter Twenty-seven

Lunch was served in a small conference room behind the Senate meeting room in the Capital. Judge Davidson, his wife Lillian, Peter, Mark and Etta had ordered sandwiches from the senate dining room, and they were eating in silence when Etta answered a knock on the door. A uniformed Senate police officer asked to see Judge Davidson. Samuel invited him to come into the room, "How can I help you officer?" he asked.

"I would prefer to speak to you alone, sir, would you mind coming outside for a minute?"

They were gone only for a minute or two. Lillian asked what that was all about but received no answer. Samuel finished his sandwich, reached into his pocket and pulled out what looked like an advertisement until he turned it over so everyone could read it. The background was a large cross in black with red printing that said, "Death to the Jews", nothing more.

"It was found on the floor of the meeting room after we

recessed, obviously placed there by someone who was in the gallery this morning. They wanted me to cancel this afternoon's session but I refused. They also wanted to have the gallery closed and I refused that as well. Rabbi Ross has agreed to be questioned later and the guards are going to do individual searches and pat downs before we start. I would prefer that you did not stay, Lillian, or you either, Mark. The guard will escort you to a limo and you can wait for me at the hotel."

Lillian shook her head no and said so in a loud, firm voice. "If you stay, Samuel, I stay, nothing more to talk about."

Samuel knew that conversation was over. He just smiled to himself. They were about to celebrate 60 years together and she would have no part of a separation over a threat to his life. He took her hand, squeezed it in his and they walked out of the room together.

Peter looked Mark square in the eyes and grinned, "Once a warrior always a warrior, Mark. I saw it in my father and I see it in yours."

Chapter Twenty-Eight

The afternoon session began promptly at 2. Samuel had always been a stickler for beginning on time. Why should we punish those who are prompt, was his question whenever he was asked why he felt compelled to begin his court sessions and meetings exactly at the time they were scheduled?

"We will hear from Rabbi Arnold Ross this afternoon. I have known the Rabbi for more than 50 years. My family was a member of his first congregation, he taught my children Torah and Bar Mitzvah, and I studied the Mishnah with him on Sunday mornings. He is the author of several books and a consultant of Jewish thought in the National Council of Churches and Synagogues."

Neither Lillian nor Mark had seen Rabbi Ross in several years and they were impressed that he looked so vigorous and alert, almost eager to answer questions as he sat in front of the microphone.

"Well, Rabbi, I am pleased that you are here and I would

like to ask you, do you believe in Intelligent Design and, if you do, what is your definition of ID?"

"Yes, Samuel, forgive me, sir, yes, Judge. I do believe in Intelligent Design."

There was a discernable gasp from those present and the photographers raised their cameras as if on cue and began snapping pictures.

"Order, please!" Judge Davidson shouted over the din as he rapped his gavel until the photographers sat down and then he asked, "And what is Intelligent Design, Rabbi?"

"My studies, my faith in God, my questioning of our very existence has led me to several conclusions about how we came to be on this Earth. My first conclusion was that God is an extremely complex and wise, for want of a better word, entity. That in his wisdom he envisioned a place, a paradise, a Garden called Earth that he would create and inhabit with creatures of all kinds. So in the realization of his wisdom he created Earth, where he placed all the elements that would sustain life as he envisioned it.

"And he gave his paradise earth, in and of itself, the intelligence of Nature. Through nature, life on earth evolved, all life on earth evolved. God knew that humankind would join the animal and plant Kingdom when the earth was ready to sustain human life. He knew that man would have free will with the ability to think, and act, and reason. He knew because he placed all of those elements on earth too to be a part of humankind. His supreme intelligence is what I call intelligent design."

The entire room was stunned by Rabbi Ross's pronouncement. A look of astonishment was on every persons face.

"Then you do not believe God created man, Rabbi?"

"Not in his image as it is believed. God created the elements and environment for man to evolve, to live. There is no doubt in my mind that a supreme intelligence created all that inhabits this earth. Just as George Washington is the father of our country, God is the father of all of us. He created the atmosphere where man could evolve and we have, unfortunately."

"Why do you say that, sir?"

"Just look back in history. At some point in time, our ancestors joined in small groups and cognized a creator, a father figure. They called that figure God. Some societies had a God for every activity, every emotion: war, love, food, envy and even gods that controlled the weather. Their beliefs became their way of life, their religion. You know as well as I do, Judge, from the beginning man created an image of God, what He looked like, what He thought, what He wanted and then killed those who did not accept their beliefs."

"Rabbi, as usual you astound me. How do you feel about the proposition of teaching ID in schools, of using the Bible as a text book?"

"I only know the Bible that I read and study. It is not a textbook of science or scientific discipline. It is the religious and national history of the people of Israel as they searched for God and a moral way of life. To read the Bible as a textbook is unthinkable. The Bible, in my opinion, is not historically correct and needs interpretation of events that may or may not have happened. It is more of a guidebook than a book of historical facts and should be read as that.

"There is no conflict between religion and science as I see it. They are two separate realms; science asks the question how and religion asks the question Why? Science deals with answers derived from experiments and religion deals with values and standards of human behavior. Albert Einstein said; *Science without religion is lame. Religion without science is blind.* Further, he stated, *I cannot conceive of a personal God who would directly influence the actions of individuals, or would directly sit in judgment on creatures of his own creation. My religiosity consists in a humble admiration of the infinitely superior spirit that reveals itself in the little that we, with our weak and transitory understanding, can comprehend of reality. Morality is of the highest importance-but for us, not for God.*

"So my answer is a resounding no, we cannot teach the

religion of a majority just because it is a majority; we cannot and should not teach religion at all in public schools. Religion has been and is the primary cause of hatred, war, and separation. It is territorial and loaded with demands and religion makes promises that are unsubstantiated, that has not, and may never be fulfilled. In my view, the primary purpose of life is connectivity, connectivity to all creatures, human and otherwise that inhabit our planet. Religion separates us."

"Do you have any suggestions as to how we can change that condition, Rabbi?"

"I do, Judge Davidson, but is this the proper time and place to reveal them?"

"Perhaps it isn't. Do you have anything else to say before we adjourn?"

Rabbi Ross shook his head no and Judge Davidson continued, thanking everyone for attending and closed by announcing that due to some serious threats made to him and the people who had spoken, and to those who were scheduled to speak, that the remaining forums would not be open to the public.

The reporters stood and began shouting questions and snapping pictures. Samuel asked them to call him individually, and he might give them a private interview. He took Lillian by the arm and left quickly. Rabbi Ross and

Mark joined them and they drove away in a government van.

Reporters and photographers were jostling for position on the stairs in front of the Capital, waiting for Senator Flowers to appear. As he approached the exit door his cell phone rang, he answered it, nodding his head up and down as he listened, then snapped it shut angrily and walked out into the bright sunlight.

"Senator, Senator, Adam," rang out from the crowd below him. He was grim faced and taut, his fingers curled into fists as if he was ready to strike someone when his aide put up her hand asking for silence. "No questions today. There will be a press conference in the Senate media room tomorrow at 10, credentials only, no photographers." Adam and his entourage walked quickly to their SUV's and drove away.

Chapter Twenty-nine

It was a beautiful fall evening in Washington. A light breeze cooled the air; the leaves were changing color on the hills in the distance. Lillian asked the driver if he knew of a seafood restaurant where they could sit outside and was not too far away. He said he did, picked up his cell phone, made a call then turned the van around and headed for the Potomac a few minutes away.

Mark started to say something but Samuel signaled him not to talk. He had to assume that his father knew he was going to question Rabbi Ross and did not want the driver to hear the conversation. They rode in silence, arrived at the Maryland Crab Cake, and were escorted to a table on the porch.

"Just what I wanted," Lillian said.

When the waiter left, Mark turned to Rabbi Ross and said, "I was a bit taken with your agreement about Intelligent Design, Rabbi. It just didn't seem consistent with what I have always known about your views."

"I am very glad to hear that, Mark. If you were surprised then I have to assume that others were, too. I just could not see a Jew dissenting about our Christian friends' beliefs without giving their political purposes more ammunition. What I said did not entirely refute their understanding of God. It did give me an opportunity to talk about finding a common denominator that might heal the schism that has been apparent for over two thousand years.

"We Jews do not doubt the wisdom of God, his supreme intelligence. We have been seeking answers about our existence for 5600 years. The Christians and Muslims have been fighting for domination of mind and territory for 2000. They number 3.4 billion, more than half the population of the world we are only 12 or 13 million. We supplied answers in the past- we must supply solutions in the present to secure a future. They advertise and market their wares as promises for an afterlife. We don't advertise and have only one identifiable symbol.

"When they wanted to kill us, and they have wanted to for generations, they pulled our pants down to see if we were circumcised. Convert or die. Most died. Constantine was brilliant when he created the cross as a symbol, for him a sword, for the then few Christians, a reminder of a crucifixion that blamed the Jews for the killing of their savior. The word should be "Crucifiction," for the story has never been true but it sold well.

"At least now we have a nation to call our own. Aside from the fact that the Arab League, all Muslims, issued their "Three No's," in 1967, no to recognition of Israel, no to negotiations with Israel, no to peace with Israel, we have an obligation to live according to the tenets we find in the Bible. However, domination of mind and territory is again at stake. What civilized, educated, intelligent being can hold an entire people in hatred for an act that they did not commit 2000 years in the past? My speeding ticket of 5 years ago does not make my son guilty of being a speeder, too. And all of this because of how they interpret God; my God is better than yours, loves me more, has a place reserved for me but not you.

"If Israel is threatened, and it may be, if war in the name of Love of God, comes about, the world may very well go down in flames. I am sorry if I seem like I am on an old soapbox. I wanted to say those things today but it was not the right time, or right place. We must present a reasonable, acceptable solution to the hatred between religious people of all faiths. The beginning of that plan can only start when Jews, Muslims, and Christians can agree that we are all a part of God's Intelligent Design of Nature, not of Man, of Nature. That every tree, every mountain, every blade of grass, every animal, every plant, every human, is as one in the eyes of God. Then and only then can we live on Earth in the Paradise that we inhabit."

"Where do you start, Arnold, where do you start?" The words seemed to come from a distant place, not from the lips of Samuel. It sounded so forlorn, so impossible.

"Start with Adam," Lillian said in earnest, her face a solid mask of sincerity. "Who better?" she continued. "He has the faith of a Christian and the blood of a Jew. Hitler would have killed him for being Jewish, the crusaders too, regardless of what he claimed. That is where you start. Convince him that faith of mind does not alter the reality that we all have the same Father; come from the same place, our blood is interchangeable. Make him understand that we are at the crossroad of humanity; we need a new paradigm of consciousness, a common thread to bind us together."

Chapter Thirty

The phone call Adam received was from the President, who was furious. "The last thing I need now is to be tied to you and your stupid remarks, Adam, and I will be. I have called for the Inner Circle to meet tonight for damage control. Be here at 8."

By 5 that evening it was on every channel. "Senator says, if I believe it, it is true," came from CNN. "Evidence not important, faith becomes fact," came across on Fox to the surprise of many. Finally, Bill Broz, a reporter on CNBC stated, "We now know how decisions are made by the leaders of our government today. Senator Adam Flowers, long an influential, intimate member of the President's inner circle, has stated that evidence supporting Intelligent Design is not necessary, that if he believes it is a fact, then in fact it must be so. I have long suspected that many major decisions regarding the war in Iraq were made without regard to evidence contrary to what the President told us. Now I know, and you do too. It seems the dominant force in

American politics today is Fundamental Evangelical Christianity. That force elected the president in 2000 and 2004 along with their majority in the Senate.

"I can well understand now why we have constantly refused to believe the scientific evidence of global warming, pushed for drilling for oil in the Alaska Wildlife Sanctuary, paid absolutely no attention to fiscally responsible tax cuts and gone to war in Iraq. Those fundamental Evangelical Christians are responsible to the American people. Those in power believe that the Earth as we know it will soon disappear because it says so in the Bible, and they firmly believe that the Bible reflects God's words. There is no evidence that God exists, but it is a fact. There is no evidence that heaven exists, but it is a fact. There is no evidence that Jesus loves them, but it is a fact.

"We in the media have long shied away from confronting those in politics with questions regarding faith and religion. It is time now to take off the gloves and ask hard questions, demand factual answers., The very least we can do, as far as I am concerned, is to find out from our sitting president if what Richard Nixon said "When the president does it, that means that it is not illegal," is true. The End of Time believers must be held accountable now. As my hero, Edward R. Murrow used to say, 'Good Night and Good Luck'.

The morning newspapers spared no one. Editorials across the nation were consistent in their criticism of the policy makers in Washington and the narrowness of their stand. Several wrote editorials condemning the 45 Senators and 186 House members who received high performance marks from the Christian Coalition, Eagle Forum, and Family Resource Council. Others took to task the many Christian fundamental groups who believe that concern for the environment is irrelevant because Earth has no future-because we are living in the End Time when the Son of God will return, the righteous will enter heaven and the sinners will be condemned to eternal hellfire.

Chapter Thirty-One

The Senate Media room was filled to capacity at 9. Television monitors had to be installed in the hallways to accommodate the throng of reporters covering Senator Flowers' 10 AM press conference. The enormous interest was sparked by a late evening press release from the White House that read, "The President, on the advice of the Attorney General, has suspended indefinitely the hearing on Intelligent Design being conducted by Judge Samuel Davidson."

Promptly at 10, Senator Flowers, followed by his aides and known press and security people from the White House, entered the media room. Sally Parker, the Senator's press secretary, took the podium and announced, "Senator Flowers will read a prepared statement and then take a few questions. We are limited in time due to a newly scheduled emergency budget meeting of the Armed Forces Committee this morning. Senator Flowers."

Adam, nattily dressed but looking drawn and tired,

approached the dais without his usual bounce and swagger. He reached for the microphone, pulled a few sheets of paper out of his breast pocket, adjusted his reading glasses, and in a shaky voice, began to read, "Good morning, members of the press. It seems that a few of my remarks yesterday caused quite a stir in the media across the country. That they did surprised me, because you who have followed my career have always known how I feel about my religion and my hero, Jesus Christ.

"Now, for the first time in American history, I can say that the majority of our Congress, the leadership in the White House, businessmen and a plethora of Christian leaders believe that we are living in End Times, that the prophesies of the Bible are within reach. There are those among us, such as Doctor Adam Grant, also a Texan, but now an educator in Tennessee, who said,

'Christian politics has as its primary intent the conquest of land—of men, families, institutions, bureaucracies, courts and governments for the Kingdom of Christ. I believe that Christian domination will be achieved by ending separation of church and state, replacing U.S. democracy with a theocracy ruled by Old Testament law, and cutting all government social programs, instead, turning that work over to Christian churches. We must abolish government regulatory agencies such as the U.S Environmental Protective Agency, because they are a distraction from our goal of Christianizing America, and subsequently, the

rest of the world. World conquest, which is what Christ has commissioned us to accomplish. We must win the world with the power of the Gospel. And we must never settle for anything less. Only when that conquest is complete can the Lord return.'

"So, ladies and gentlemen of the press, you now know the agenda that our leaders in the Congress and the White House are pursuing. I am in complete agreement with those policies and support them whole-heartedly. If you have any questions, I will take them now."

The first question came from a seasoned reporter from Washington: "We understand that you met with the president and other members of the Republican leadership last night to discuss your remarks of yesterday afternoon. If that is so, sir, does the statement you just read reflect a consensus opinion of those you met with or just your own?"

"The information you have about a meeting is correct. There will be no comment on the second part of your question."

A young reporter in the rear of the room stood without being asked and said, "When I was a young man, my hero was General Douglas MacArthur. When he left the Philippines in 1942 he said, 'I shall return'...and he did. I tried to live my life as he lived his. I believe that is why we have heroes, sir. So my question is have you emulated your hero during your lifetime, and do you have any proof that

Jesus will return?"

Adam, white faced, visibly shaken, stared at the reporter who had been very friendly and supportive of him in the past and said, "No to both questions," turned away and left the podium. Sally quickly announced, "Senator Flowers' meeting is about to begin. Thank you for coming. This press conference is concluded."

Chapter Thirty-Two

Mark sat alone in contemplation in his hotel room, wondering what course of action he might take with Adam Flowers when his cell phone rang.

"Rabbi Davidson? This is Jack Fox of the *Times*, how are you?" Mark was not aware that his cell phone number was available so he asked him how he had obtained it.

"Peter Carmody gave it to me."

"How do you know Peter?"

"I interviewed him last year after I met him at a book signing. Great guy and a fine writer, he has been an inspiration for me."

"For me too. What can I do for you Jack?"

"I am trying to contact your father but can't reach him at his home number. Do you know where he is staying and would you please give me his number? I want to schedule some time for an interview."

Mark hesitated then remembered his Dad's invitation for the reporters to call him. "He's at the Watergate and will be there for a few more days. Best time to call is early morning before he goes out for his walk. I'm not sure he will have time for you but you can try. Nice talking to you and good luck."

Fox thanked him and said he would be in touch. It wasn't fifteen minutes before Mark's phone rang again; it was his father calling, "Mark, I have given Jack Fox Thursday morning to interview me. I would like you to be here, too, if you can make it. Just don't trust those newspaper people but don't want to have Etta take notes; Fox might be insulted. Anyhow, we will start around nine if you have time."

"Of course, not a problem, are you still going to write a report?"

"Just my personal views. It should be finished Wednesday; I am not sure it will be happy reading for many people, especially the President and his cronies, but I have to say it as I see it. I am really too old to worry about consequences. Your mother isn't happy with it but I am. See you Thursday, son, and thanks."

"Dad, are you sure you want to release it to a reporter before you give it to the president?"

"Thought about that; the president will have it on Wednesday. I am going to hand deliver it to the White House at his request. I don't really know this man in the White House, and I don't trust him. My intuition tells me that he will sit on the report, may not release it, or will use it as political ammunition in '06. I don't want that to happen, so I will tell him I am going to be interviewed on Thursday and that I will talk about my personal views on any question that I am asked. I don't think he can deny me that, so unless he puts a legal gag order on me I am free to speak my mind as long as I do not give the paper a copy of my report. I think it would hurt him politically if a reporter stated that a gag order was issued that forbade me to express my personal opinions, don't you?"

Mark laughed in wonderment at his father's reasoning and told him so before he hung up.

Mark was in the lobby of the Watergate hotel when Jack Fox approached the reception desk. It was exactly nine o'clock. Judge Davidson, always prompt, walked down the corridor from the elevator at the same time and greeted Mr. Fox, "Good morning, Jack, always glad to meet with people who are on time." Mark joined them and they were escorted to a comfortable conference room on the far side of the huge lobby. Coffee and pastries were on a side table and an attendant was in the room to serve them.

When she left, Jack turned to Samuel and said, "My editor was contacted late last night by the White House press department. They did not threaten but they did make it clear, that in view of the fact that the hearings were postponed they did not want any interview with you published in the paper. How do you feel about that, Judge Davidson?"

"In forty years on the bench I never talked about a case before it was adjudicated or afterwards until all avenues of appeal were exhausted. That is a rule of law, not a personal opinion. But this is not a law case, Jack. I have opinions that I have had for years on the subjects I heard at the hearings. I have read the books, letters, and essays written by those who graciously appeared before me. So, I can and will answer any questions you might want to ask without worrying that my answers may or may not be in the report I made for the president. That is his problem, not mine. I came to this at his request as a private citizen, he knew that I might write a report that he did not favor and I think I have, but I know I have a right as a private citizen to express my thoughts and philosophies to anyone I wish to. You can begin anytime you are ready, sir."

"Are you going to write a report, Judge?" he asked.

"Yes I am, Jack. I want the president to know my feelings regardless of who spoke, or didn't."

"Do you believe in God, Judge Davidson?"

"Yes and no, Jack. Ever since man first appeared on this Earth, he has been searching and praying to something of his own making. The ancients of Greece and Rome had their

Gods, many of them; Aphrodite and Zeus as the God of all Gods among some that they worshipped. The Egyptians had Pharaohs and a multitude of gods as did the Incas and other indigenous people throughout the world. No civilization ever existed that did not have mythical icons to worship, to bring good fortune, protection from enemies, and favor for war. The wise men of those eras created Gods to explain nature, to help them identify and live with the unexplainable. Those civilizations died out and the wise men of the next generations created their own Gods to worship. Then came the generation of seekers five thousand years ago and we are their descendants. That is when other groups of elders created their Gods to help them, including Jesus Christ.

"Men created the myths and stories that we in our civilized generation now worship and have worshipped for thousands of years. The world was thought to be flat in those days. Medicine and science could not explain how life was created. Much of what we take for granted today did not exist then; it has evolved. It is interesting for me to ponder how the thoughts and deeds of one man who lived two thousand years ago could capture the faith and have such influence on humankind of today.

"What I am trying to say, Jack, is this. The thoughts of one man became the dream of another and the reality of still another. All that we know in science, medicine, and religion emanated from the thoughts, doubts, and inquisitiveness in the mind of one man. In science, hundreds of years apart, one man pursued his quest for energy; Faraday's experiment led to calculations and a formula that defined the speed of light. Year's later mass was explained by a French experimenter. Then those formulas resonated in the mind of Albert Einstein and from his formula came the splitting of the atom and the release of energy in overwhelming amounts now used for weapons and fuel. Medical advancement follows the same path and religion must too.

"Every civilization had its thinkers and philosophers. The religions and Gods of yesteryear disappeared as civilization progressed. Monotheistic thought has brought us through the days when man believed he must conquer nature. Today we must think that we are Nature. If, as I believe, God created Nature then we are God, too. It is hard for me to think otherwise. Can there be one God for all six billion humans on Earth? I do not think so. Nevertheless, I can believe that God exists in every one of us. And we must believe that we are all connected in Nature if we are to survive.

"So the religion of today must change, must evolve from the multi-Gods to the many Gods, to the one God, which have separated us for thousands of years. We still fight wars in the name of one's true God. The age of God may be over unless we change our consciousness and the era of oneness in Nature

begins. It may be that man, who has searched for God for so long, may have it wrong. What could be reality is that God has been and is searching for man that he envisioned, and that evolutionary thought, the thought of connectivity, may very well be the catalyst that saves humanity forever. Or at least for generations until the next period of life begins on this Earth."

Fox then asked, "How do you feel about Iraq, Judge?"

"Many years ago a brilliant young man, about 35, received his doctorate in religion and became a minister, a preacher. He had a dream one night that he had the knowledge and vision that could save the world. His long journey and failure to achieve that goal led him to a smaller one; maybe he should just save his country. He labored on that for 15 years to no avail. Then he settled on his state and failed, his city and failed, his neighborhood and failed. Then, at age 90, near death, he had a revelation: if he only had become himself what he envisioned for the world he would have influenced his family, they the neighborhood, the neighborhood the city, then the state then the country then the world. That is what I think of America, Mr. Fox. Perhaps when we reach maturity and we become what we want the world to be, we will have earned the right to be emulated."

"So Iraq was wrong, sir?"

"Based on the reasons we were given, yes."

"What do you think should be done, Judge Davidson?"

"I don't know. Jack. What I do know is this; what we are telling the world to do we are not doing in America. Wars are generally fought between nations. When one Army kills enough of the enemy, the government surrenders and sues for Peace. There is no entity in Iraq to sue for Peace, Jack, we either must leave or stay. Neither is an option."

Chapter Thirty-Three

Mark read Samuel's report on Wednesday afternoon paying particular attention to the religious references and comments for context and clarity. The report's length, only two pages, and the simplicity of language impressed him. When he commented about that Samuel answered, "It has to be understood by everyone who reads it, Mark."

This is what Judge Davidson took to the Oval office and handed to the President.

Dear Mr. President,

Although the hearings were cancelled after only two people had spoken, I felt compelled to write my thoughts and feelings about Intelligent Design from their viewpoint and mine. The two men who appeared before me were intelligent and passionate about the subject of Intelligent Design. Adam Flowers was firm in his belief that the Bible was the Word of God to be read and followed as if it were historical fact, taught in schools, and that Christianity should be adopted as an official State religion. He is prepared, as he put it, "To use

Congress and the Courts to change the American culture." The Senator did not think there was a conflict between teaching ID, Creationism in schools as it makes no reference to God as the creator and is consistent with the separation of Church and State. When asked about proof of his belief, he expressed his Faith in God as reason enough.

Rabbi Ross had another viewpoint entirely. His views encompassed a Universal view of Humanity, of oneness. That we have too long been separated by organizational entities we call religions, especially Christianity.

As for myself, sir, I believe that Christianity has overly influenced America from the beginning and that influence is at its apex today. To further a religious agenda by teaching Intelligent Design in public schools without scientific evidence is a violation of the Constitution. I have spent an entire career pursuing justice and making decisions based on physical evidence and the law. I therefore cannot condone the teaching of one group's faith as an absolute or as an alternative to what evidence, science presents.

I present this to you, Mr. President, as a very concerned and informed citizen for your use and dissemination as you see fit and respectfully thank you for the opportunity to be of service to you and my country.

Most respectfully,

Samuel Davidson

Chapter Thirty-Four

Peter and Mark were having lunch at the Washington National airport before flying to New York. Mark had a disturbed look on his face when he said, "I was getting a haircut this morning, just sitting in the chair thinking about what we could do to influence Adam, when the barbers started to talk about their ancestors. I generally don't pay any attention to the conversations in a barbershop but I was curious, then furious with what I heard. One of the barbers, a woman who used to cut my hair exclaimed quite loudly, 'I am really mixed; one of my grandparents was Italian, another German, another was French and one was a Jew.' After spending the week listening to all the religious talk at the ID hearing, then reading my father's report, religion and the inherent religious differences that separate humans, I had to ask why she had identified three of her grandparents by nationality and one by religion. She stammered, was silent for a minute or two, and finally said, 'I don't know.'

"What is it that makes people separate Jewish people

from others, Peter? This isn't a new phenomenon, you know, but I certainly would like to see it become an old one."

"I guess you Jews fulfilled your purpose on earth when Joshua was born, Mark, so now you have to find a new place to live or give in."

Mark looked at him and smiled. Peter always knew how to break the tension.

"I guess we need a new advertising agency", Mark responded grinning. "The message that we don't drink Christian blood or have human sacrificial orgies hasn't gotten across yet."

"Do you have any ideas for a campaign, Mark?

"Roses are red, violets are bluish, if it wasn't for Christ, then everyone would be Jewish. Kindergarten stuff, but the first thought that popped into my mind."

"That's a start, my friend, but let's get serious. Judaism is one of the only major religions that don't follow the teachings of an individual. The other is Hinduism. Think about it, Buddha, Confucius, Mohammad in the East and Jesus Christ in the West. Could it be that those who follow a teacher are wary of those who don't? It bothers me, too, has for years and it isn't enough to say 'some of my best friends are Jewish', either, even though you know that it's true. So what, some of the most hateful people I know are fervent followers of their Christian/Catholic faith and they can't tell me why they hate the Jews as much as they do. Christ killers don't cut it after 2000 plus years even if it had been true."

"Peter, some of my colleagues are beginning to express the thought that Judaism is more of a way of life than a religion".

"You're serious, aren't you?"

"Of course, the talk is that the Torah is a guide book, a way of life with historical references. I am not saying that I believe them but what is religion if it is not a way of life? I played tennis with a Florida state senator once whose name was in the papers because his daughter was arrested for selling drugs. He asked me, more in the form of a statement than a question, 'How could this be happening to me, I live such a good Christian life?' I just did not have the heart to ask him what the difference was between a good Christian life and a bad one. Oh how I long for the day when we don't make reference to what country we live in, how we worship or where our ancestors came from when we talk about people. Just see them as we see ourselves."

"Wishful thinking, Rabbi, wishful thinking. But don't stop, you have a direct line to the Master, I have to go through an intermediary."

The boarding announcement for their flight temporarily terminated their conversation as they entered the line at the gate. When they were seated and the plane began to roll down the runway, Peter turned to Mark and said, "Matthew is going to meet with Adam and show him the letter tomorrow. If Adam is receptive, I may fly down in a day or two to meet with them and talk about getting together with your family."

Chapter Thirty-Five

Jack Fox's interview with Samuel Davidson appeared in the magazine section of the *Sunday Times*. It was short and concise. "That you are reading this is a tribute to the publisher and editors of this newspaper. I have been on the staff for nearly forty years and never once in all of those years, in any of my stories have I allowed my personal feelings to get in the way of my doing my job. But after attending the ID hearings and the Senator Flowers press conference, I began an investigation into End Time thinking as described by the Senator. It seemed to me that a good place to begin was the Internet and I was right. Following and reading a myriad of articles I wound up at this web site. Portions of the article that intrigued me are published below. I must tell you it infuriated me to read it and ponder the minds of those who propose, support, and pray for "Rapture" as they call the end of the world, as it is prophesized in the Bible

This is what Glenn Scherer wrote in his column at
http://www.grist.org/news/maindish/2004/10/27/scherer-

Christian

Many Christian fundamentalists feel that concern for the
future of our planet is irrelevant, because it has no future. They
believe we are living in the End Time, when the son of God will
return, the righteous will enter heaven, and sinners will be
condemned to eternal hellfire. They may also believe, along with
millions of other Christian fundamentalists, that environmental
destruction is not only to be disregarded but also actually
welcomed -- even hastened -- as a sign of the coming Apocalypse.
Like it or not, faith in the Apocalypse is a powerful driving
force in modern American politics. In the 2000 election, the
Christian right cast at least 15 million votes, or about 30
percent of those that propelled Bush into the presidency. And
there's no doubt that arch-conservative Christians will be just
as crucial in the coming election: GOP political strategist Karl
Rove hopes to mobilize 20 million fundamentalist voters to help
sweep Bush back into office on Nov. 2 and to maintain a
Republican majority in Congress, says Joan Bokaer, director of
Theocracy Watch, a project of the Center for Religion, Ethics,
and Social Policy at Cornell University.

Because of its power as a voting bloc, the Christian right
has the ear, if not the souls, of much of the nation's leadership.
Some of those leaders are End-Time believers themselves. Others
are not. Either way, their votes are heavily swayed by an
electoral base that accepts the Bible as literal truth and eagerly

awaits the looming Apocalypse. And that, in turn, is sobering news for those who hope for the protection of the earth, not its destruction.

Ever since the dawn of Christianity, groups of believers have searched the scriptures for signs of the End Time and the Second Coming. Today, most of the roughly 50 million right-wing fundamentalist Christians in the United States believe in some form of End-Time theology.

Those 50 million believers make up only a subset of the estimated 100 million born-again evangelicals in the United States, who are by no means uniformly right-wing anti-environmentalists. In fact, the political stances of evangelicals on the environment and other issues range widely; the Evangelical Environmental Network, for example, has melded its biblical interpretation with good environmental science to justify and promote stewardship of the earth. But the political and cultural impact of the extreme Christian right is difficult to overestimate.

"All over the earth, graves will explode as the occupants soar into the heavens," preaches dispensationalist pastor Matthew Hagee, of the Cornerstone Church in San Antonio, Texas. On the heels of that Rapture, nonbelievers left behind on earth will endure seven years of unspeakable suffering called the Great Tribulation, which will culminate in the rise of the Antichrist and the final battle of Armageddon between God and Satan. Upon winning that battle, Christ will send all unbelievers into the pits of hellfire, re-green the planet, and reign on earth in *peace with His followers for a millennium."*

Many years ago, a friend of mine introduced me to his "religious grandparents," who, whenever they were asked about the future, proclaimed, "Armageddon's comin'!" And they believed it. Christ was due back any day, so they never bothered to paint or shingle their house. What was the point? Over the years, I drove by their place and watched the protective layers of paint peel, the bare clapboards weather, the sills, and roof rot. Eventually, the house fell into ruin and had to be torn down, leaving my friend's grandparents destitute.

In a way, their prediction had proven right. But this humble apocalypse, a house divided against itself, was no work of God, but of man. This is a parable for the 231 Christian right-backed legislators of the 108th Congress. Their constituency's beliefs may lead to the most dangerous and destructive self-fulfilling prophecy of all time.

"What infuriated me most about this article and others I read is the strength of faith these people have and their utter lack of concern for other people including non-committed Christians and the staggering loss of life for the 'Good of Humanity.'

"I cannot fathom the God that would sacrifice 6 billion people, their hopes, and dreams, for the sake of a few million who claim to be the Faithful, the True Believers, and

The followers of Jesus. How un-Christian is the murder of billions in the name of one who died on the cross? In my mind, the actions of Hitler are akin to the kindness of Mother Theresa in comparison to the desires and aspirations of those who preach the End of the World in the name of their savior. As a reporter, I can no longer be silent. As a human, I can no longer be silent. As an American, I can no longer be proud for this all seems to be coming from American Christianity. As a Jew, I can assure you that these so-called thoughts of Jesus are not the actions of those who call themselves Christians.

Jack Fox.

Chapter Thirty-Seven

Matthew was in charge of public relations, marketing, and advertising for the Committee to Advance Christianity in America, CACIA as it was referred to within the Republican Party. His co-workers called him SS for two reasons, one, a reference to Senator's Son and the other to his relentless pursuit of his focus on the party's agenda. He read newspapers from across the nation before breakfast every morning, scanned the Internet for hours looking for negative press and publicity and for opportunities to advance the cause.

His recent pursuit led to a behind the scene investigation by the Internal Revenue Service of an Episcopal Church's tax-exempt status after a sermon criticizing the Iraq war and the proposed tax cuts for 2010. Working closely with the NAE, National Association of Evangelicals, Matthew arranged for a full hour at prime time on NBC to espouse their philosophy. Praised by his superiors, he continued to work for the inclusion of prayers in schools, the teaching of

Intelligent Design, and creating a National Religion for America.

He had dedicated his life to Jesus Christ from the age of 20 and kept his focus intact with daily prayer sessions and bible classes. Now, at the age of 30, after spending time with Peter, examining the position of those in charge of the party and the White House, and hearing from Connie about her brother-in law Alan Rothman. Matthew felt that it was time to reexamine his life.

Alan was a career Air Force officer at the Air Force Academy teaching combat flight tactics. His refusal to attend mandatory Christian prayer sessions led to disciplinary actions by his superiors. After going through channels, he met with and complained to the Commanding General. Shortly thereafter, Alan was transferred, passed over for a promotion, and given an unfavorable mention in his service record. Publicity from his treatment led to an Inspector General's investigation and report that Christianity was over emphasized at the Academy to the detriment of cadets and officers of other faiths. Several of the officers in high positions were criticized and transferred. Alan, under tremendous pressure from his fellow pilot officers, resigned his commission and left the Air Force.

Matthew had doubts about what he was doing from time to time, but his devout faith in Christian principals sustained him. The only times that he had approached his father in the past were when he needed counseling about religious issues of ethics and morality. Adam always had time for him when these issues were paramount. It hadn't been so in the past as Adam was so focused on his own life that he had little or no time for his children.

Chapter Thirty-Eight

When Adam was in Washington, he and Susan lived in a Town House in Georgetown. Small by his standards but quite comfortable for the two of them, it was dominated by a great room library on the first floor. Adam had moved much of his grandfather's book collection from the Austin house when he was elected Senator and had remodeled his new home extensively. Only a large kitchen and bathroom were on the first floor with the library. Two master bedroom suites and a den were on the second floor.

Matthew had a key to the town house and often came by unannounced for breakfast. But he needed to know his father was home so on this particular morning he had called ahead to let Adam know he was coming over. He read the Post in the taxi and was surprised to read about an Israeli official coming to Washington to discuss the election of Hamas in the Palestinian territory with American Intelligence Agencies. Her picture was on the front page.

Matthew opened the front door, called out "Father,"

picked up the morning paper, entered, and walked into the kitchen.

"I'll be right down, Matthew, have a cup of coffee."

"Who is Sara Brodsky, Dad?" Matthew called out.

"Who?" Adam shouted.

"An Israeli, Sara Brodsky."

"Never heard of her, Matthew," as he walked into the kitchen. "Should I know her?"

"She knows you, father. Mentioned your name in today's Post. She is here to brief Intelligence Agencies and said she was looking forward to seeing you again. Here is her picture," as he handed the front section of the Post to his father.

"Well, I'll be damned, that is a picture of Sara Richmond. I knew her in college, years ago, haven't thought about her for thirty years."

He took the paper, walked to the window, and stood there muttering for several minutes before he poured a cup of coffee and sat down at the table with his son.

"Well, Matthew", Adam began, "we haven't had much time together lately, have we?"

"No, sir, we haven't. But that's the way it always was."

"Are you complaining, son?"

"In a way, yes, I am." Matthew replied.

"I did too, Matthew. My father never had time for me

either and, it seems, his father for him. My grandfather was a hardnosed one-dimensional taskmaster. Money and religion were his gods and Jesus was his master. He passed the religious traits to my father who passed them on to me and I guess I passed them on to you. Hard work and prayer, praise the Lord made for a purposeful life, Matthew but not a very happy one; at least not for me."

Matthew was taken aback by his father's response. "Getting soft in your old age, I guess," Matthew replied, "I never heard you talk this way."

"I should have gotten closer to you years ago, son. I saw so much of me in you. But I didn't and I regret it now."

Matthew was about to say something when Adam began speaking again.

"I was a very good athlete as a youngster but I never really played for the right reason, to have fun. It was always for the reward promised and given by my father or grandfather for results. Tennis titles came first and with them money, a horse, then cars and even women after I turned 18. I had little regard for those I played against, Matthew, they were the enemy. I traveled with a coach, lived like a hermit, and was constantly prodded to win. I looked at other players having fun and derided them in my mind as fools. I didn't realize it then but all of my contacts were fervent Christians until I went to college.

"The Flowers family trust endowed a chair at Texas and donated a lot of money to the school so I was a known entity when I enrolled. I do not know it as a fact, but suspect that my roommate was vetted and chosen by my parents. My roomy left school after the first year and I lived alone until I graduated. Having a small apartment alone was a major gift when it came to parties and I liked to party, Matthew. Beer and liquor were hidden behind futons in a hall closet and the futons were put to use often. Flowers Fun Fests were a monthly tradition until I met Sara. She was a cheerleader from Dallas who came to my apartment with a football star, looked around and left. She was tall, blonde-haired person, well shaped with long thin legs and a beautiful smile. I sought her out on campus and introduced myself to her at the cafeteria.

"I fell in love with Sara Richmond and after a month or two, she with me. I stopped drinking and concentrated on my studies. I went to the football games that I had not done before to watch her, the game itself was incidental. I was head over heels in love and I bought a ring to give her on Christmas. As I think back now we never talked about the future in those first months, we just spent all of our time together enjoying the moment. I was 21, she was 19. I stopped going to church on Sundays and she never mentioned anything about religion. In my mind everyone was Christian, what else was there? I guess she didn't care one way or another.

"I took a job teaching tennis at the Dallas Racquet Club that summer to be near Sara. She worked as a lifeguard at the swimming pool. I met her parents; her father was a lawyer and a good tennis player. We played a few times and for the first time in my life I was enjoying myself in everything I did. The Pastor of the First Church of Christ, a member of the club and one of my students, asked me to come to church one Sunday and I asked Sara to come too. She said, 'Of course I will come with you, Adam, but you do know that I am Jewish, don't you?'

"I didn't know, never gave it a thought. I was blind for a moment or two, my mouth went dry and when I started to speak no words came out. She asked me if I was all right. I nodded my head, yes, but I wasn't all right, Matthew. I wanted to scream, I was in love, madly in love, making plans in my mind to become engaged, and now she tells me she is Jewish.

"When I recovered enough I told her I would see her later and went back to the tennis courts. I had a group lesson scheduled and had to hit balls and talk to 12 teen agers. I hit them much too hard for them to reach and spoke much louder than I had too and they were perplexed about my behavior. The rest of that day became a blank until I picked

Sara up at 6 that evening. She was waiting for me outside of the gate by the swimming pool and walked toward me as she usually did, and then reached out and took my hand and we walked away as we had been doing for three weeks."

"Why didn't you tell me you were Jewish, Sara?"

"You never asked and what difference does that make anyway?"

"What difference does it make?" I shouted, "I come from a family that hates the Jews. They killed Christ."

"Do I look like a killer, Adam?" She asked. "Isn't it kind of weird and infantile to blame someone for something that might have happened two thousand years ago?" Her voice was so quiet, so innocent that I felt ashamed.

"I love you, Sara, I want to marry you," was all I could say.

"And I love you too, Adam, but I won't make any commitment to you about marriage until I finish school."

I was a year ahead of her and could not think of waiting two more years without knowing if we would get married. "You will convert, won't you?" I asked.

'Convert?' she said, 'to what and for what reason? I am a decent, thinking, caring human being whom you loved a few hours ago when you didn't care what else I was. If becoming a Christian is a qualification for me to be with you for the rest of my life then we had better stop seeing each other right now, Adam. I love you for what I see, what I know you are as a person, not for something or someone you worship. That something is a wall, will always be a wall between you and me and everyone else that feels superior because they believe Jesus loves them. There is absolutely no way of knowing that Jesus even knows if you exist let alone know that he loves you."

Chapter Thirty-Nine

"I tell you now, Matthew, if she had agreed to marry me at that moment I may very well have become Jewish. We continued to see each other until Sara graduated and I asked her to marry me. She said yes and agreed to meet my family in Austin. It hadn't occurred to me until that moment that my father might object unless she converted to Christianity, and even then he might not agree. I was prepared for resistance but not for the totality of his ultimatum.

"When I called and told my father that I was bringing a girl home and that I was going to get married he was pleased. He asked me her name and I told him Sara Richmond. He hesitated for a moment and then asked 'is she Jewish?' My heart started to pump and when I said yes he asked me if she was going to be baptized. When I said no he told me that I had better come home alone until we talked. There was no anger in his voice just a firmness that made me think I had a real problem. Sara understood, since she had told her parents about me early on, something I guess I should have done too., Her parents had voiced their concerns but didn't object, but that was not so in my case.

"My grandfather had died the year before I graduated and left me some money in a trust. I had the ability to withdraw a small sum at twenty- one, which I did, a larger amount at twenty- five and the balance in full at thirty. The total amount was enough to make me financially independent so I knew that I could stand up to my father if he threatened to cut me off if I married Sara. I told Sara this before I left for Austin and promised her that we would be married as planned. Obviously that didn't happen.

"On the plane home I thought about my mother. I wished that she were still alive; she had died a year before, just after my 21st birthday and had been a buffer between my father and me. Now that she was gone I only heard my father's words when I left to play tennis in New York and New Jersey as a much younger man. 'There are a lot Jews out there, Adam, don't ever forget what they did to our Lord Jesus. Be wary of them don't get too close to them, Adam,' and I never did.'

"I have to tell you son, I was not looking forward to that meeting with my father. He was never easy to talk to about politics, money, or religion when my mother was alive. Now he was drinking heavily, was very abusive to his nurse/attendant, and had no contact with the outside world.

His life was close to how Howard Hughes lived in his later years, reclusive and suspicious of everyone. I hadn't seen him in nearly a year and I was shocked at his appearance, thin, very thin. His eyes were sunken into his head, he was wearing a beard, and he looked like he was a hundred years old and ready to die. But his mind was as sharp as ever.

"Well, Adam,' he greeted me, 'now that you want to get married, you don't think you need your father's permission do you?'

'Not your permission, sir, just your approval,' I answered.

'Wrong, Adam; you need my permission if you want to receive your inheritance from your grandfather's trust and be the recipient of my will when I die.'

"He seemed to be taking pleasure in telling me this and I was not prepared for what I was hearing. As a matter of fact, I was very angry and he knew it when I shouted at him, 'what do you mean?'

'There is a provision in your trust that I must approve anyone you choose to marry and another provision in my will that voids it if you marry a Jew even if she converts to Christianity. I hate them Adam, and had hoped that you would, too. They are born Jews, live as Jews and die as Jews, that never changes. They may convert but they never change and Adam, you must believe that as I do if you want my money.

"I made a mistake, Matthew, I gave into him. Not at that moment, the next day at breakfast. I spent the night thinking about the future, my future. I was out of school, never had had to work for money, didn't like the idea of being poor or starting from scratch and enjoyed all of the pleasures and freedom that money gave me. It wasn't the religion or the hatred that influenced me, Matthew, only the money. I wasn't the Christian then that I am now. When I returned to Dallas and told Sara I wouldn't marry her she asked me why. When I told her she said, 'Narrow minded men like your father will eventually create an impenetrable wall between people that will destroy the world. And you, Adam, will never know the happiness that the freedom of your own mind and your own purpose can bring.'

"In a way she was right. I missed her, Matthew; she had lightness about her, intelligence and an inquisitive mind. I called Sara from time to time, even drove past her house once or twice. When I read that she had married I stopped thinking about her. I started on a six-year binge though that nearly destroyed me and, in fact, killed three of my friends. That was when I discovered the real Jesus and began a career that brought me honor, recognition, and direction.

"The Forester family were our neighbors and Susan, their daughter and I loved horses. They had a big spread, not as large as ours but big enough to ride for hours. We rode together often. I was attracted to her even when I knew Sara. She was lively, fun- loving, and very comfortable with the Forester money. Every year after Sara and I split I asked her to marry me. She always said no. 'Maybe when you stop drinking and carousing,' was her answer until I proposed to her when I returned to Austin from rehab.

"I passed my love of Jesus on to you and now you are passing that knowledge on to others across the nation. You can't imagine how proud that makes me as a father, a Senator and a Christian, Matthew. I admire you and I love you for who you are and what you are doing, son."

Chapter Forty

"Will you see her, father?" Matthew asked.

"See who?" Adam said as if he had already forgotten the conversation.

"Sara."

"I never look back, son, never ponder what if. No, I won't see her."

"What about Connie?"

"What about Connie?" Adam answered angrily.

"She is your daughter, sir. You should see her."

"She stopped being my daughter when she defied me, Matthew."

"She didn't defy you, Dad, she honored you by following her heart and mind just as you wanted to do but didn't because you were not strong enough."

Adam was standing up, pacing back and forth, his anger glowing in his red face, "But she is no longer a Christian and that is intolerable to me," he shouted at Matthew and continued walking around the large room.

"Please sit down, Dad, I have something to say to you and I can't concentrate if you're walking around like you are."

Adam was perplexed but did as he was asked. He glowered at his son as he sat in the red leather chair opposite Matthew.

"For the past four months I have been questioning my beliefs, my work and my religion, Dad. It started with a meeting I had with Connie and..."

Adam was livid when he exclaimed, "You have seen Connie even though you know how I feel?"

"She is my sister and she had something important to show me that concerns us all. I'll get to that in a few minutes but I have to take my time and tell you what is in my mind before I do. Along with what she told me she gave me a book to read called *Constantine's Sword*. That book took me a month to read and really shook me up. It traces the history of Christianity and the perpetuation of anti-Semitism throughout the world that exists even today. Reading it produced a strange thought in my mind: instead of asking the Jews to apologize to Christians for killing Jesus, we Christians should be asking forgiveness from them for all the killings and misery we have inflicted on them for so long.

"For years I have been reading *Left Behind* books,

believing what the author said and wrote about, and raising money for the National Association of Evangelicals. Now I question the fundamental Christian's belief in Rapture when all of the Christian followers will leave this Earth and live in Heaven while all non-believers will perish and be doomed to Hell.

"Now I question the truth of the Virgin Birth, that Jesus loves us. I don't like the idea that we support Israel as a national homeland for the Jewish people until Christ returns and Rapture happens. It is incomprehensible to me now that the blood of billions of people will flow like rivers. That the return of Jesus will signal the beginning of a Christian world and America will become the New Jerusalem."

"Who have you been talking to, Matthew, who has been poisoning your mind?" Adam asked. "Obviously they must be Jews and liberals who do not know the truth."

"One of them is your daughter, sir; two others are a rabbi you know and an ex-priest. They haven't poisoned my mind, just asked me to open it and stop being blind to other people, other religions, and other ideas.

"Connie returned recently from the devastated area of Pakistan where she was a volunteer emergency care worker. She went with a group from New York to help where help was needed, in remote villages. They were the first people to arrive in a small village five weeks after an earthquake. They treated hundreds of people as best they could and with limited resources. One man, the father of a seriously injured young girl, squatted in front of Connie and asked her to sit down in front of him. He spoke no English but put his hands in front of him fingers spread wide and gestured to Connie to do the same. When she did he counted his fingers and then hers, then touched his arms and legs then hers, saying in sign language, 'we are all the same.' I cried when she told me the story.

"I am still not convinced that we are all the same from birth to death. I just want to have my family back again as a family. I want us to recognize that God makes no deference to man but man makes deference to God based on the teaching of man, that that teaching may not be based on the truth."

Adam saw that all of this was very difficult for Matthew but he was also curious about what prompted Matthew to talk like this. "What isn't the truth, Matthew? He asked.

Matthew stared at him for a few minutes before he responded, "You are not the truth, Dad, and I am not the truth, nor is Connie."

"And just what does that mean?" Adam asked in a very sarcastic manner.

"Dad, I promised Constance that I would not tell you what we found out until we are all together as a family; you,

Mom, Con and me."

"That can't happen," Adam bellowed.

"Then you won't know, might never know," Matthew whispered. "Connie is waiting for my call; she has a ticket and can be here in the morning. It is your choice, sir."

Adam began pacing again; he reached for a cigar but did not light it. He looked at family pictures on the piano, recent pictures of Connie had been removed but one of her as a child in her mother's arms still stood. Adam picked it up, paused and turned to Matthew, "What time?"

"She is booked on the shuttle and can come any time you say."

"Make it early," Adam said and walked out of the room.

Chapter Forty-One

Matthew stood by the gate anxiously watching the ramp for signs that a plane was arriving. The ground crew started moving at 8:05 and the plane was attached to it 5 minutes later. Connie was the first passenger to enter the terminal. Matthew greeted her warmly, took her overnight bag and looked her over. She was wearing a flowing skirt and baggy sweater especially selected to hide the first signs of her pregnancy. "Don't want Dad to know, eh?"

"Not yet Matthew, maybe I will tell him, maybe I won't. Have to see how it goes."

"Nervous?"

"Very."

The cab ride took 15 minutes. Matthew used his key to open the front door. The smell of fresh coffee greeted them as they walked through the narrow hall into the breakfast room. John Shelby Spong's book was next to the coffee pot on a side table. The bookmark was near the end and small pieces of paper were sticking up throughout the pages. The table was set, bagels, butter, and cream cheese sat next to a plate of smoked salmon. Too obvious, Matthew thought, and smiled as he looked over at his sister. She was smiling too as Adam entered the room. He shook Matthew's hand and pecked a kiss on Connie's cheek. "Are you well?" he asked. The question was not really a question that required an answer so Connie nodded and sat down quickly. She told Matthew later that she was shocked at Adam's appearance. He looked like he hadn't slept in a week. His eyes were tired, large dark circles surrounded them, his hair was disheveled and he had gained a lot of weight since she had last seen him three years ago. She also confessed that her knees began to buckle and she had to grab the edge of the counter to keep from falling.

"Coffee?" Adam asked as he poured a cup and offered it to Connie. She pushed his hand away and said, "Tea, if you have it." Adam had water boiling on the stove and a container of various teas in a cabinet over the coffee maker. It was obvious that he had thought about this morning and seemed to be prepared for anything.

Matthew started to say something as he reached for the breadbasket full of bagels but thought better of it. 'No need to bring up a Jewish thing at this moment,' he thought. Connie took half a bagel, spread some cream cheese on it sparingly, added one slice of salmon, poured hot water over a tea bag she had selected and waited for her father and Matthew to sit down. The silence hung heavy in the room until Matthew asked, "Good book, Dad?" as he pointed to Spong's book on the counter. Matthew had read it and suspected the answer before it came.

"The guy's a nut," Adam responded. "I stayed up until two this morning and then didn't sleep because I was so angry."

"He's been a bishop for more than 20 years. He must have given it a lot of thought before it was published and he is still a bishop. That says something, doesn't it?" Matthew had had the same reaction when he read it for the first time a year ago but when he read it again after his conversations with Connie, he had to agree with some of what he had learned.

"He's still a nut, Matthew, and will always be if he believes all of the crap he writes about."

Connie looked up and saw anger all over Adam's face and a twinkle and sly smile on Matthew's face. This is a prelude she thought and Matthew has him where he wants him.

"Church attendance is down, Dad. Why do you think that is?" Matthew asked.

"Maybe in your church, and for sure in the Catholic Church, as it should be. Who wants to expose their children to unmarried gay priests? Not in mine though, it is soaring. Attendance is way up and the National Association of Ecumenical's now has about seventy million members. We have power, real power with goals that will make America stronger and better. In the four years that I have been on the Board we have had access to the White House as never before. It won't be long, Matthew, when we will be able to elect Presidents, Senators and Congressmen with little or no opposition. This country will be the light of the world and we all will have Jesus to thank."

Connie whispered quietly, "God forbid."

"And when Rapture comes the Earth will be uninhabited, the graves of believers emptied, the Heavens filled with joyous, dancing Christians chosen by the Board of the NAE. Is that what you are waiting for, Dad?" Matthew was angry, determined, and forceful. "Sara was right when she said you would have no joy in your life. You are looking to a future life at the expense of the only life you will ever have right here and now. There is a wall that separates us all by what we were taught not by what we are, but what we listen to every Sunday, what we read in the Bible and take literally. Your grandfather, your father raised you to be like them, narrow, prejudiced, and fearful of God. And you raised Connie and me in the same mode. Connie feared you and I emulated you. But we have moved on, we see life from a different perspective. I can't speak for my sister, only for myself. I submitted my resignation to the Republican Party last week. I am taking a year off to live in Israel and discover my roots, my Jewish roots."

"Your Jewish roots? Where did they come from might I ask?" Adam was perplexed, angry and very sarcastic.

"From you, Father," Connie answered, "from you."

"We didn't want to tell you like this," Matthew interjected, "we wanted to have a conversation, not a confrontation. It just seems to happen every time we get together and it is always over religion. First, when Connie married David and now when we have spent the last five months trying to find a way to break the news to you that Barry was not your father and Kate not your mother. Those five months have been extremely trying for me, Dad, and I have never done so much soul searching or reached such disparate conclusions. Con, can I continue or do you want to take it from here?"

"You're doing fine, Matthew."

Adam had calmed down, lit a cigar, poured a third cup of coffee, the shocked look on his face had disappeared and he was listening intently.

"Dad, you are half Jewish, your father was a Jew, your mother a devout Catholic."

"That makes sense, the Jew taking advantage of a

Catholic woman and I am the result" Fire came from his mouth as he raged at Matthew.

"No father, not even close, actually almost the opposite," Connie stated. "Your father was a fighter pilot stationed on Iwo Jima and flying 8 hour missions over Japan. On July 8, 1945, he was over Tokyo and his tent mates, and his classmates, were killed. He was distraught and your mother, a USO performer at the front to sing and dance, consoled him and made love to him as a supreme gesture of giving. You were created in a moment of genuine love, one human to another. Your father is Samuel Davidson and your mother was Kate's first cousin Pat Meisenger. She died six months ago and we learned about this from her attorney who forwarded a letter she had written a month prior to her death in June of this year."

Adam looked stunned, couldn't speak for a long time, when he recovered enough he asked, "How do you know this is true?"

"We have a copy of the original birth certificate," Connie answered.

"Is it still on file?" he asked.

"No, it isn't, Barry had the original replaced on the day after you were born."

"Then how do you know this is so?"

"Connie and I had DNA tests done with blood from

Mark and Samuel Davidson," Matthew answered. "The tests were conclusive, we are related."

"Oh my God, oh my God," was all Adam could say as he put his hands over his eyes and slumped down onto the table.

It dawned on Matthew then that their mother, Susan, was not at home. He was bewildered and went upstairs to see if she was sleeping. He searched the house and found no evidence that she was present. When he returned to the kitchen Adam was sitting at the table, coffee mug in hand, staring out of the picture window toward the Washington Monument. He didn't look up when Matthew asked him, "Where is Mom?"

"She is at Betty Ford getting over an addiction to sleeping pills," he answered. I am going to Palm Springs on Sunday to see her."

"Why didn't you tell me?" Matthew asked with a slight bit of anger in his voice. "I might have been able to help you. Do you want me to go with you Sunday?"

"Thanks for the offer, Matthew, but no. I really would like to be alone now, Matthew," he said as he rose from the table, "I'll call you in a day or so. I need to think."

"But Dad, we need to talk, we need some answers."

"Not today," he said abruptly

Matthew looked at Connie, she handed him an envelope

and Matthew placed it on the table. "Here is the letter, Dad, and a copy of the birth certificate. I also put some new phone numbers with them, as I am moving. In case you want to contact Connie her numbers are there, too."

They said goodbye, Adam just nodded and they walked out into the bright morning sunshine. It was 9:30; they had only been there an hour, a very long and stressful hour.

Chapter Forty-Two

Adam, alone in the house, walked idly from room to room, deep in thought. Why isn't Susan here when I need her was his first thought? Where was I when she needed me? They were married for 32 years, 32 years that followed his priorities: religion, politics, wife then children in that order. He hadn't paid much attention to her nightly glass of wine to swallow the pill she kept next to her bed. He wasn't concerned when the wine became vodka and one pill became two. Her daytime behavior became erratic, unpredictable but he wasn't at home much and when he was he wasn't really there.

The phone was in constant use with calls from colleagues, ministers, and fundraisers. Susan cooked and served meals almost every night and never paid attention to who she was serving. They must have all looked alike to her, the talk and laughter, lost from her reality as she became more dependent on alcohol and pills. Adam was in Tucson at a golf outing when she collapsed. She was taken to the hospital in Georgetown; her condition was very serious and would require long time care and rehabilitation.

She had been at the Ford clinic for two months now, not the few weeks he had told Matthew and Connie. There was no telling how long she would have to stay in rehab and Adam needed to talk. He knelt in prayer and prayed for guidance and direction. He received no answers to his prayers just questions that he himself would have to answer. He spoke aloud, "I don't want to be alone, I have lost my children, my wife is ill, I need to talk, what can I do, what should I do?" He felt better as he always did when he finished and stood up. He saw the envelope that Matthew had placed on the table, picked it up, fingered the metal clasp then replaced it on the table. The kitchen was a mess; he busied himself cleaning up, put the dishwasher on then went upstairs to take a shower. He was lost in memories of his youth as he shampooed his hair. He recalled his matches for the National Junior championship and the NCAA championship against Mark Davidson. Why these thoughts now, he asked himself when I have so many problems to solve?

Mark, the Rabbi, he had called him. My God, he thought as he stroked the razor across his cheek, my God, he might very well be my half-brother if I can believe Matthew and Connie. He was startled by the thought that maybe Mark might be a person he could approach for information about this situation. No, he thought, that will not work, I would not know how to approach him or what to say.

He packed a bag on Sunday morning, put Matthew's envelope in his brief case, and called for a cab. He left the house at 11 for a 1 o'clock flight to Los Angeles. He checked in at the Admirals' Club, took a seat at a window overlooking the runway, opened the Manila envelope, and read the letter twice. It contained so much information that he decided to let it sink in and not think about it until he reached Palm Springs. The plane left on time, he settled into his first class seat, leaned back, and closed his eyes. He usually slept on long flights but sleep did not come this time. Questions kept popping into his mind, should I tell Susan, would she comprehend, can I tell my colleagues, the press, what will the reaction be by my Texas backers, should I just drop it, will it be leaked next year when I am up for re-election, should I call Mark, or Samuel or Connie or Matthew. Somewhere over Middle America, he reached for the phone in the seat back in front of him, swiped his American Express card, and called Matthew.

Chapter Forty-Three

Mark knew that Matthew and Connie had met with Adam. Peter had told him just a day after their meeting but he had no idea what Adam would do.

"What do you think Adam should do, Dad?" Mark asked when he called his father.

"No way to predict, son" Samuel replied. "I remember when Madeline Albright found out that her families on both sides were Jewish. She was the Secretary of State, raised a Catholic, and, as I recall, she said nothing, nor was much made of it in the press. Of course, she hadn't been an elected official nor was she known for her religious views as Flowers is. At best, if it does get out, and it might, he will be the one who makes the decision about what, if anything, he wants to do."

A few minutes after he hung up the phone rang. Mark was surprised when he picked up the telephone and heard Adam's voice.

"Mark, this is Adam Flowers."

"I take it that you have read the letter, Adam," he replied.

"Yes, I have and I need to talk to someone about it. Are you available?"

"I am or could be but are you sure you want to speak to me?"

"No, I am not. Actually, I am not sure of anything at this moment. But I do need to speak to someone about...about this matter and thought you might be best. My son Matthew thinks so too, I spoke to him about it a few minutes ago and he gave me your number."

"I have to tell you, Adam; I have been thinking about this for five months, you have only known about it for a few days. I may not be the right person for you to meet with right now."

"I know you never liked me, Mark, and that you don't respect my political views and aspirations. But I had nothing to say about how and why this situation came about nor did you, in that regard we are even. Whatever I do or say will reflect on you and your family as well. If I had to say something to the public right now it might not be flattering or even responsible, just an emotional reaction. I don't want that to happen and I suspect that you don't want that to happen either. So we should talk."

"OK, Adam, when and where? Would you mind if Peter

Carmody was present?"

"I will be in Palm Springs for a week and can be in New York for a few days on the way back to Washington on January 10th. Why don't you check with Carmody and see when he is available and let me know."

"I'll be in touch, Adam, after I speak to Peter. What number can I use to reach you or would you prefer email?"

"No emails please, they become public material and I don't want any record at this time. Just use this unlisted cell number. By the way, I might ask Matthew to join us." He gave Mark his cell phone number and said goodbye.

Chapter Forty-Four

Adam arrived at the Betty Ford clinic at 10 for his meeting with Susan's therapy team. They told him they were pleased with her progress but wanted to make sure that he did not upset her routine or mental state. "Her addiction," they explained, "came from a frustration with not being able to communicate honestly with you and your inability or unwillingness to give her time or listen to her attentively. That is the reason we have not let you see her or speak to her for the past two months. You may find that she has changed some; she is more assertive and unwilling to be shunted away when she has a need to express herself. You can help her tremendously, Senator, by letting her express her views, even those that are contrary to yours."

Adam was on the patio across the street from the administration building when Susan came walking towards him. She was wearing pink shorts, a white blouse and sandals. She was striding confidently toward him then slowly began to run until she grabbed him around the neck and kissed him. Even at sixty, the juices flowed after a long absence. Adam hadn't experienced such an enthusiastic greeting in years and he responded warmly.

"You look great," he said.

"I feel even better, Adam. It's so good to see you, hold you; thanks so much for coming."

The strength in her voice made it known to Adam that he could share his story with his wife. Perhaps I won't want to meet with Mark Davidson after all, he thought. They moved from the patio area to the coffee shop nearby. Sandwiches and iced tea were ordered and Susan told him that she had spoken to Connie and Matthew the past week.

"Did they tell you that I saw them, too?" he asked her.

"No," she said, "they didn't mention that. But did you see Connie too, Adam?"

"I did," he told her, "but only for a brief time. They wanted to talk but I needed to be alone. You know how it is."

"Only too well, Adam, only too well." Her voice saddened, she stared out across the desert landscape, wiped a tear from her eye with the back of her hand, took a sip of water and looking Adam square in the eye, spoke firmly.

"Adam, I am over the physical addiction, you know what that is like, but I may never get over the mental abuse you have put me through, and unless I do, our life together is over."

Adam was startled by the sound of her voice and the words even though he had no comprehension of what Susan was saying. "I don't understand what you are saying, Susan. I thought you loved me."

"With all my heart, Adam, that will never change, but I can no longer go on playing third string in your life. Everything was fine until you ran for the second term in 2000. You and the Texas Mafia became obsessed with getting elected and pulled out every stop, legal and otherwise and did what you set out to do. But you lost your daughter and nearly lost your wife in the doing. I never questioned your ardor, Adam, just your methods. And, dear husband, I never believed in the war we are mired in now. I faced those years for the first time head-on these past months, and now that you are only a month or so before gearing up for re-election, I must face you with my anger and indignation intact. You haven't even told me why you finally allowed Connie and Matthew a few minutes with you after scorning her for three years and then dismissed them to get ready for a meeting. They are your children, damn it, and they come, always came, last when it came to your needs. I am shocked that Matthew has such respect for you after years of neglect by his father."

"That may be changing, Susan, Matthew is going to Israel for a year to, as he put it 'find his roots,' his…

"Christian roots, Adam, how wonderful it will be for him to walk where Jesus walked, Adam."

"Jewish roots, Susan, Jewish roots," Adam said sadly.

"Since when does he have Jewish roots, Adam? Surely he means the Jewish roots of the Lord?"

Susan was a questioning Christian. Her faith in Jesus was absolute but not always in the same mind set as Adam. They argued about the Bible often but without resolution. "How can God free the Jews from Egypt, part the sea, protect them from plagues, give them the Ten Commandments, make them his people, and then have them kill Jesus so Christianity is created in His name?" was Susan's main theme. "The Catholic Church created ghettos, exiled them and killed them by the thousands, Adam, where is the logic of calling Him the King of the Jews and keeping them subjugated to the cross and the sword?"

Adam never had any problem arguing forcefully, that "God moves in mysterious ways, Susan, we cannot know what He has in mind for us other than to follow Jesus faithfully as written in the Scriptures until we reach Heaven and find the answers."

As always, Susan was wearing her large silver cross as she and Adam talked that day in Palm Springs. The sun reflected light from her cross into Adam's eyes and he was squinting badly when he said, "I am half Jewish Susan.

Barry wasn't my father nor was Kate my birth mother. Read this," and he handed Susan a copy of the letter and birth certificate.

A half hour passed before Susan could speak. Her first words were questions, "So what does this mean to us, Adam? How will it change our life? Or will it?"

"I'm not sure I have an answer, Susan, just your questions and more. I called Mark Davidson, Rabbi Davidson, and he has agreed to talk to me next week. The only thing I have in common with him is that we have the same father.

"Don't we all Adam?" Susan asked.

"Don't we all what?" Adam responded testily.

"Have the same Father."

"So did Cain and Abel, if that means anything."

"Are you planning on running for re-election, Adam?"

"Not only planning but they want me to be the new majority leader. They think we can keep the majority in the Senate if we disconnect from any legal problems or potential lawsuits any of our current people have. Some of my Texas friends want me to take a softer view on Iraq and I have been thinking about it. Not because I agree but that's what the public seems to want. Damn it, Susan, I didn't need this disruption now. My loyalty has been to our Christian principals, we are closing in on our goal of overriding any constitutional objections to a national religion, and now this."

"This is an opportunity, Adam, darling. It is God's way of telling us that you are a Universal man, a part of all religions. If you are going to be re-elected, Adam, you will have to be up front about this revelation. I do not think it will be a negative if you reveal it, but it could be very damaging if you do not and the papers print it. As for me, well, I just hope that this will open your heart and mind to the qualities that Jesus was born with, came to us with and died with and stop following the quest for fundamental Christian domination of the world. Our country needs to re-connect, stop the internecine struggle for domination and control. How wonderful it would be if you could find a means to have the American people create agenda items for the President and Congresses approval. And ways to make sure that all Americans are the beneficiaries of the actions of Congress, not just the majority party or the favored few"

"Good thoughts, Susan, good thoughts. If I could find an answer I might want to make a run for the Presidency in 2008."

"Oh, Adam, why is it that everything we talk about becomes something for you and nothing for me?"

Adam looked up at her with curiosity as if he really did not understand the words as Susan continued.

"Where are we right now, Adam? At a picnic, enjoying the Riviera? No dear husband we are at the Betty Ford Center for alcohol and drug rehabilitation named for the wife of a politician like you who escaped from her egocentric, politician husband just like I did."

"Now wait a minute, Susan."

"No Adam, I won't. You don't know how close I was to taking my life three years ago. It was the day after Powell spoke at the UN, after Dick and Rummy, Tony Blair and the President declared that we were forty-five minutes away from a 'Mushroom Cloud.' No one, not even those who knew better ever asked, 'How are they going to deliver it, in a suitcase?' I had the note written, the pills on my nightstand. I stood there for a few minutes, thank God the phone rang. I thought about not answering it. Fortunately I picked it up, and it was Connie.

"Mom, she said, it's Connie, I have some news"

"I sat down on the bed, held the phone away from my ear not knowing what to say."

"Mom,' she said, 'are you there?' You're a grandmother.'

"We didn't even know she was pregnant, Adam. Connie, I shouted, how wonderful. Are you all right?"

'I'm fine,' she answered. 'Oh, Mom, how good to hear your voice.'

"I started to cry, she did too. Your granddaughter is three

years old, Adam, her name is Sara. I wanted desperately to hold her, to hug my daughter but I couldn't. I couldn't bring myself to go behind your back then but I will see her now with you or without you. That's what I want, Adam, to be a mother again, to see my grandchild grow up, to have a family."

Adam, shaken, stood up, paid the check, took Susan's hand and asked, "How long are you going to be here, Susan?"

"That's up to you in a big way, Adam. I can go home now, this week, but only if I can assure Doctor Jaffe that you will be there to support me. He wants to meet you and I said I would ask."

"Of course I'll meet him. I will do anything, Susan, anything. I need you too, now more than ever."

Two days later, they left Palm Springs for New York.

Chapter Forty-Five

Mark met Adam and Susan in their suite at the Waldorf Towers. The concierge on the floor was expecting him when he walked off the elevator and escorted him to the door, rang the bell, bowed slightly and left before a uniformed attendant opened the door. So this is how the ultra rich live, Mark thought, as the butler took his coat and hat, placed them on a chair and led Mark down a short hallway to the dining room. The table was beautifully set for three; Adam rose from his seat, walked toward Mark his hand extended. He took his guests' hand firmly and spoke up in a low, gentle voice.

"I am extremely grateful that you came here today, Mark. This is my wife Susan." Susan stood up and smiled.

The warmth of their greetings made Mark feel at ease and he responded, 'I am very glad to meet you, Susan, and to see you, Adam.'

Adam motioned Mark to sit and asked if he would like something to drink.

"Whatever you are drinking would be fine with me," Mark answered, knowing that Adam hadn't had a drink in over 30 years and that Susan had just been released from Betty Ford and he did not want to embarrass them. Iced tea was served and Adam raised his glass and said, "To the beginning of a friendship."

Adam smiled and nodded his head when Mark clicked his and Susan's glasses and said, "Welcome to the family."

Mark had thought about this moment from the first minute that Adam had called. He had decided he would not initiate any conversation, just respond to him. Adam seemed friendly but Mark didn't trust him. Susan was very quiet throughout the lunch and Adam, acting the host, made sure that everything was to everyone's liking. Lunch over, they moved to the living area for coffee and dessert.

"When did we first meet, Mark", Adam asked, "thirty, thirty five years ago?"

"Something like that", he replied, "at the Nationals, 14 and under. You creamed me in the singles but Peter and I beat you in doubles."

"I didn't like losing, then or now, and I let you know it didn't I, Mark?"

"Yes, Adam, you did," wondering where he was going with his questioning.

"I especially disliked you because you were good, and..."

"Where are you going with this, Adam? I knew the reason why then and now so why don't you just say what's on your mind?" Mark was abrupt and somewhat angry and didn't like himself for it but it was too late.

Adam looked at him with cold eyes before he started to talk.

"I was five, 1951, when I heard the word "Jew" for the first time. My father was talking to my grandfather and he was very angry. I remember him saying, 'that Jew Rickover is going to destroy our business. Once they put atomic submarines in place, the whole goddamn Navy will stop buying oil. I'm spending thousands of dollars a week in Detroit and Washington making sure that they make bigger, heavier cars and don't allow imports from Japan or anywhere else to flood our market. Now this Rickover has convinced the Navy that the future lies in atomic energy.

"I asked them what a Jew was and they told me someone who killed Jesus, and doesn't believe he is the Lord. That was the beginning, Mark."

"When I went into the Texas legislature my father reminded me quite vociferously that I was to keep Flowers oil in my mind and make sure that I did everything I could to keep energy efficient programs off the books. The few liberal Jewish officials who wanted clean air and price controls on oil were my enemy. When Nixon made Kissinger his Secretary of State my father was livid. I never took to him either even though he was brilliant and, from all outward appearances, loyal to the President and the party, just because he was a Jew. Altruism never entered my mind when it came to profits for Flowers Oil Company. Still have that in my mind now when prices are kept high and profits are soaring for American producers. Then, Connie and Matthew gave me the letter written to your father."

Adam stopped talking for several minutes. He walked out of the room, returned with a pitcher of coffee, offered a cup to Mark who declined, poured a cup for himself, and started to talk again.

"I have to tell you, Mark, I was startled. I reacted badly and dismissed my children when they needed to talk. I guess you knew that I hadn't seen Constance for three years and never expected to see her again because she married a Jewish boy against my wishes."

Mark was listening to every word, looking for clues, to see if there was any softening of his anger and noticed he said "Jewish" instead of "Jew."

"This is very hard for me, Mark," he said.

"I expect it is, Adam, Mark replied, "It isn't easy for me or my family either."

"What is most difficult for me is my position in the Senate and the Republican party; where I stand and what I am promoting for our country. I have..."

"Adam, I don't want to talk politics with you; religion, yes, politics, no. I will leave that to my brothers and father if, or when, you meet with them. For your information, Lee has lived in Japan for twenty- five years and left America because he thought it was out of control then. Jay is an extremely liberal Democrat and actively protests the actions of the current administration and Alan is a voting Republican. My father and I share the same views as Jay and I will leave it at that for now."

"But Mark, my life is politics and religion. I can't separate the two."

Mark hesitated a few minutes, mulling through an answer to his statement. Several thoughts entered his head including ending this conversation and leaving. 'Let him talk' seemed to be best at the moment, so he asked, "What do you mean by that?"

"My family has supported the Republican party for generations. It wasn't until Kennedy was elected in '60 that the party saw the possibilities of bringing their religious beliefs into politics. If they could elect a Catholic to the presidency, we could elect a fundamental Evangelical Christian and bring our views to the forefront of American life. Be a power, change America back to what we knew the founders always wanted, a God- driven democracy. It took forty years but we have done it. I can't let our country go backwards, Mark, I can only help America become greater by staying the course we started in 2000."

"It doesn't sound like reading your birth mother's letter has changed anything for you, Adam."

"You may be right, maybe it hasn't." There was sharpness to his voice that seemed to come about abruptly. Susan started to speak but did not when Adam glared at her, "What I believe seems to be more important than whose blood flows through my veins. I didn't realize that until I saw you again, Mark. You reminded me who and what I really am and what I will always be."

Susan had started to wipe away her tears as Mark stood and thanked her for the lunch and started to leave their suite, angry for letting this conversation get away from him.

As he left the table Susan, in a firm, sure voice stated, "Life is not a tennis match, gentlemen. One does not live for rewards or winning records. One lives to fulfill God's gift to humanity, to do what is right for everyone, not just for your own religion or political party. If the two of you can't understand and accept that then what hope can we have for the future?"

Her words stopped Mark dead in his tracts. He looked at

Adam, whose head was down, his body trembling. When he looked up at Mark, he extended his hand. Mark took it and they gripped each other's hand firmly, their eyes met and Adam nodded his head as Mark left the room.

Chapter Forty-Six

"The universality of all religions is forgiveness and thankfulness without which we cannot have faith." It was Samuel talking to Adam as they strolled along the edge of the Gulf of Mexico on the beach. Adam and Susan had returned to Fort Lauderdale from a New Year's cruise to the Caribbean and, on impulse, Adam had called Mark to get Samuel's number before they flew back to Washington.

"I may want to see him, Mark. Is that all right with you?"

"It has nothing to do with me," Mark answered and gave him the number.

You can walk for miles south of the pier on the beach at Passagrille without encountering another person. It was a favorite place for Judge Davidson to walk and he did so most mornings. Occasionally he would break into a slow jog recalling the days he would run for three or four miles on the beach in Del Mar. He told Mark later that Adam and Susan had come directly to Passagrille from Fort Lauderdale, checked into the Holiday Inn and arranged to meet him and Lillian for breakfast the next morning.

The breakfast was cordial with talk about family members, children, grandchildren and the like. When they finished eating they moved down to the beach, set up umbrellas and chairs and when Susan and Lillian were settled, Adam and Samuel left for a walk. They didn't speak for several minutes. Then Adam asked, "What do you make of the letter, Judge?"

"I was about to ask you the same question," Samuel responded. "To tell you the truth, Adam, I was upset to get it and even more disturbed when I read it, for several reasons."

They walked on kicking the surf as it rolled up the beach before Samuel continued.

"My war was clear and well defined. We knew who the enemy was, what we had to do, and we did it. The first ten years after the war is a blur. I didn't sleep well, wondered who I was, why I had lived when so many had died, but marriage and children gave me the perspective I needed and the war finally left my awareness. It surfaced again big time in 1983 when I went to Japan on business and struck me like lightening in 1988 when my son Lee got married in Japan, but I dealt with it."

"Didn't you find it difficult to forgive them for all they did?"

"Have you forgiven me for all I did?" Samuel asked.

"What do you mean, Judge? What did you ever do to me?"

"Not me, Adam, my ancestors. Hasn't the Church perpetuated the alleged crime of the murder of Christ by the Jews to this day? Doesn't your life revolve around your religion and the fundamental beliefs Christianity demands of you? Isn't the universality of all religions forgiveness? Actually, upon serious deliberation and study, I did not find the Japanese atrocities any different from any warring nation's actions, including American. Since we won that war and others, we wrote the history as we saw it. Didn't the Church do the same thing? They do not study their history in Japanese schools and I suspect you have not studied your religion's either. You might be surprised about what you might learn. The killing of Jesus unleashed centuries of killing in His name."

"Wait a minute, sir", Adam interjected, "am I responsible for that?"

"How can you ask that question, Adam, when your Church continues to preach about the Jews' complicity in that event?"

"But...."

"There are no buts, Adam, we cannot change what happened, only try and forgive and move on. And that is one of my points. Where is the forgiveness?"

"What do you think I should do ...sir?"

"Moses, like you, was not raised by his natural parents, Adam. He had to find out who he was on his own. You will, too. No one can help you, really."

A large flight of pelicans flying in formation swooped down and rode the currents in front of the breaking waves. Samuel watched them until they disappeared from sight and began to speak again.

"They remind me of my youth, Adam, as you do, too. I read Pat's letter as an 82-year-old man and felt a rush of emotions, guilt, pain, anger, frustration, you name it, and I felt it. I tossed and turned every night for a week before I realized that I had to look at this from a young man's perspective, from Pat's perspective, and that gave me resolution. That two people came together under such conditions was of itself a chance happening that could not be predicted. That they made love and created life in a place of so much death, it was and is a tribute to the powers of nature, and of circumstance that neither of us could control.

"We as humans are always responsible for our actions, Adam. But none of us has control of the result of our action. That Pat chose to talk to me, to make love on that day in that place was a gift of life for you. I agreed to see you now so I could tell you that, and only that. I have no desire to influence you, to change you or even obligate you to see life from my viewpoint. I will leave all of that to you and the people you associate with if you decide to tell them. But I want you to think before you act. In 1960, when I was thirty-six, the Republican Party was vociferous in opposing a Catholic for the Presidency of our country. Now, 46 years later, under your party's sponsorship, we have five Catholic judges sitting on the Supreme Court. Where is that going to lead us?

"You, Adam, are a man of influence. What you believe and why is your birthright. I have been around politicians for a long, long time. I have yet to meet one who has maintained his or her youthful vigor for altruism and working for the good of humanity. In my view, that must change, and soon. The events of the day are rapidly getting out of hand and we need to think American, not political party, or our country may not survive. The only progress we have made as Humans since David killed Goliath with a slingshot and a pebble 5000 plus years ago is the fact that we have invented better slingshots and better pebbles. The 1945 Pebble took 4000 years of Japanese history of a Divine Emperor out of the fantasy and myth category that gave them reason to kill, rape, commit atrocities, and start wars with impunity. Their belief system was shattered into reality. They learned that all Humans are the same. Today the belief systems of countries, individuals, political parties and the worship of deities that separate us will lead to the delivery of the next pebble that will destroy humanity."

Chapter Forty-Seven

Adam and Susan decided to drive back to Washington rather than fly. "It will give me a chance to think, Susan, What do you say?"

"You can think but I would rather talk, Adam", she answered. "We need to decide what you are going to do when the Senate convenes."

"I was thinking about contacting Sara Brodsky; get her thoughts about the Palestinian issues from an Israeli's perspective, maybe even asking Matthew to do some research while he is in Israel. It seems to me that we must solve that problem now."

Susan was perplexed and asked, "Did you hear what I said, Adam? You need to make up your mind about running again."

"Later, Susan, we can talk about that later. I need to do something now about the Middle East while I can."

"Why Israel, Adam? What happened to your plans for Iraq, Afghanistan, and Pakistan?"

"Israel is where it all began; it might be where it all ends. I need to find a way to bring people together before those things get out of hand."

"That's a change, Adam. What happened?'

"Samuel....my father is a wise old man. He said some things that...that made me think beyond what I have always thought was important."

THE END

Acknowledgment

I based this book on life's experiences, some mine, some others and some as I would like to see. Without the encouragement of friends, Tom Coates, A.J. Poulin, Neal Stannard, a fine writer and radio personality who was my editor, and Linda Egenes, I would not have sought or found a publisher. I want to thank Joyce Faulkner and Mike Angely who introduced me to Bruce Moran, of Total Recall Publications. As always, without the support of my life long partner, Helene, this story would never have been told.

Author Jerry Yellin

Was a WW 2 fighter pilot from Hillside, NJ. He flew P-51's over Japan from Iwo Jima. Married to Helene for 60 years, they have four sons and six grandchildren, three in America and three born and raised in Japan. Jerry, now retired, lives in Florida.

The Blackened Canteen

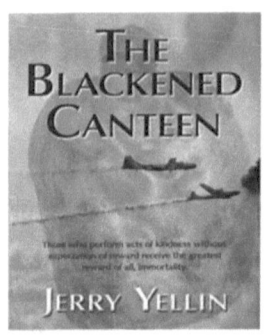

Pub. Date: September 2008
Format: Hardcover, 280pp
ISBN-13: 9781421890180

"On June 20, 1945, just before the end of the war, 123 American bombers took off from the island of Guam for an attack on Shizuoka, a Japanese city at the foot of Mount Fuji. The raid destroyed two-thirds of the city, taking the lives of two thousand of its citizens. Twenty-three American airmen also died when two of their planes collided in mid-air.

That these twenty-three men were enemy soldiers mattered little to one Japanese person who buried their remains next to the graves of the Shizuoka citizens killed in the attack and erected a memorial for them there. Many years later, in 1971, another Shizuoka citizen learned of this. He began holding his own ceremony beside the memorial, praying for the souls of the twenty-three Americans each year on the Saturday closest to June 20.

Though the two countries were once at war, the selfless action of one Shizuoka citizen over sixty years ago has built a bridge between the two countries, inspiring a campaign for peace among Japanese and American citizens, and strengthening ties between the two countries.

Having campaigned for peace for many years, this beautiful story strikes a deep chord with me. I hope it will become more widely known around the world and inspire other people too."

~Imagine Peace, Yoko Ono

"Jerry Yellin takes you from the terror of war to the everlasting hope of peace, in a unique story of World War II. -A human story like no other. God bless you, Dr. Sugano."

~ John Colli, Nephew of Ken Colli from The Blackened Canteen

"Words cannot express the true feelings of the heart when reading "The Blackened Canteen". We are brought to tears with the realization that this author cared enough to honor these fallen heroes of WWII. This fictional account has been faithfully told based on the facts of these American Soldiers lives. What a true blessing!"

~ Lucy Spence, daughter of Newton Towle from The Blackened Canteen

Of War & Weddings

Pub. Date: February 18, 2009
Format: Hardcover: 288 pages
ISBN-13: 978- 0963850256

Of War and Weddings is a moving and compelling true story of bitter wartime enemies who find peace through their children's marriage. A mysterious force that weaves its way into the lives of the Yellin and Yamakawa families ends up healing the wounds of war and nurturing a legacy of freedom and understanding for the children of America and Japan. We experience Jerry Yellin's destiny from childhood to retirement. We feel his joys, his loves, and his pains. We experience the process of healing as it occurs and are moved to discover that the legacy of two fathers is an inheritance intended for us all.

Of War and Weddings, A Legacy of Two Fathers is Jerry Yellin's legacy to his family, to his country and to the nation of Japan. The book is not just Yellin's extraordinary story of his experiences as a fighter pilot in the Pacific during World War II. it is also a story of the prejudice spawned by war and carried in the hearts of two war veterans, both military pilots, one Japanese and one American. Through the marriage of their children, the two fathers learn to make peace with their war experiences and allow the burdens of hatred for a nation and for a race to be lifted from their lives. With fascinating detail and moving honesty, Yellin navigates deftly in time between escorting B-29 bombers in raids on Tokyo in 1945, and visiting a rebuilt Tokyo on business and family trips in the 1980's. In the end, he has escorted readers on a journey which takes them through the darkness of war and brings them to the light of acceptance, understanding, and peace.

This book changed my life! I had a very distorted (and angry) view of the Japanese all these years, but this book has opened my mind to the fact that we (humans) are basically are all alike.
Written very well.
    ~ *Richard J. Medina*